The Christmas Disease

By Walt Chaney

Special Acknowledgments

I would like to thank many folks for my chance to write and complete a novel, a big goal in my life's Bucket List. Those folks – many good ones, along with a few bad ones -- have given me reason to write and find my muse, best explained by Ray Bradbury in his book *Zen and the Art of Writing*. Now I would like to acknowledge the real people in my life. My dad, Jerry L. Chaney, who made it possible for me to get a college education. My son, LTJG Joshua W. Chaney, and my daughter, Lindsey M. Chaney, the smile on my face. Cherie, my wife, thanks for playing pick-up basketball thirty-four years ago. You have made life amazing. My twenty-six years of students, for bringing laughter into my life…and, unfortunately, sometimes tears.

THE CHRISTMAS DISEASE was brought to fruition with the help of my friend, my colleague, my writing coach and my editor, the gifted English instructor and author, Ed Buhrer.

Thank you personally for the purchase of this book. Please enjoy.

Chapter 1 Open the Window

April 15, 2018 - 1000 HRS

"Dern. I have the diarrhea!"

"What? snickered Ed as he watched Wally rock back and forth in apparent stomach pain.

"Seriously! I ain't gonna make it, and this tour bus ain't stoppin' for two more freakin' hours!" Wally gasped as he bent over in his seat, holding his stomach.

Showing no sympathy for his classmate, Ed snickered, covering his mouth. "You stupid goof ball! Why'd you eat that greasy pepperoni pizza and down a gallon of extra caffeinated cola at that grease pit, Scotties's Pizza, before we left? That Italian stallion probably uses expired meat and cheese from the dumpster behind the nearest grocery store!" Ed growled as he smacked Wally on the belly.

"Ya slap my belly again and I'm gonna give ya knuckle sandwich!" Wally gasped. "Seriously, I'm feelin' like I could doo doo through a screen door!'" Beads of sweat forming on Wally's forehead glistened as the sunlight passed through the charter bus window.

Ed snickered, "You gotta case of la dia-ree-rrr."

"Don't try to speak Spanish now, I'm seriously gonna doo doo myself!" Wally groaned.

Overhearing the conversation, Mike said, "Wally, are ya prairie doggin'? Is the little turd about to stick his head out?!" Ed and Dalton began uncontrollable laughter.

"Well, get up an' use the toilet at the back of the bus, and you better go now or you *will* turn your *whitey tighties* brown." Ed covered his mouth with his fist as he began laughing out loud. The outburst drew looks and stares from their fellow seniors sitting in the vinyl seats on the charter bus taking the class of 2018 to Florida's Southern Baptist Resurrection theme park.

"I know," said Wally with desperation in his voice. "But all the hotties are in the back, especially Cherie…an' it's gonna stink! Everybody'll smell it!"

Ed rolled his eyes, "You don' have chance with Cheire and most likely never will, so go take your hot runny crap!" Ed snickered again. "Boy, you ain't got no choice."

Wally became even more uneasy as he continued to clench his sphincter with a tear in his eye. "I CAN'T HOLD IT ANYMORE! I'm headin' back before it starts comin' outta my nose!"

As Ed continued to laugh, both hands covering his face, Wally raced to the rear toilet, his dash bringing him plenty of attention as he bumped into a few students leaning into the narrow aisle of the tour bus. When he made it to the door, he was relieved to see the green light, indicating that the toilet was unoccupied.

"What's wrong with Wally?" Angela, one of the school's softball queens, called out after almost being trampled. Dalton announced, "Wally's gots to blow some chocolate chunks!"

"What a loser," yelled Mentiroso in his preppy pink *Vineyard Vines* polo.

Dalton fired back with a wide grin. "Hey, Mentiroso, take your oversized driver and give yourself a hole in one." Laughter broke out all over the bus, not so much at Dalton's crude humor but because Mentiroso was a huge brown-noser and disliked by nearly everyone except chickens. "Shut up, you stupid redneck!" was his best reply.

"Excuse me, boy, I like the way your little pink collar is flipped up. That's real sexy," Dalton responded, flirtatiously fluttering his eyelashes as he changed his expression to an ear-reaching grin. "We prefer the term *Appalachian Americans*!" Laughter again broke out throughout the rear of the bus.

Dalton and Mike, his seatmate, cheered for Wally as he raced to the back. "Go Wally! You'll make it! Blow it up, Wally!" A chant started throughout the bus. "Go Wally, go! Go Wally, go!"

Some girls in the back, including Cherie Morgan, the girl Wally had admired and lusted for since seventh grade, bawled out, "Oooooh, gross!"
"That's disgusting!" called out Angela.

Despite his racing thoughts, Wally had heard Cherie, and her remark cut through him like a knife. The embarrassment was overwhelming. He thought in dismay, *"Now she'll never go out with me!"* But it didn't matter at that moment as he flung the door open, nearly hitting Loren in the closest seat. Before the door had even closed all the way, he had his belt undone and was desperately pushing his pants down to his knees. "Aaah, I made it!" he gasped as he lowered himself down on the seat and a gastric explosion echoed in the tiny cubicle.

Students five rows up could hear the super fart as the liquid stool exited Wally and blasted into the metal commode. The boys within earshot began celebrating as if their home team had just scored a touchdown, but Pam, sitting beside Cherie, shrieked, "Oh my God, he's disgusting!"

Up front, Dalton responded, "What's the matta, Pam? Ain't ya ever had the diarrhea before?" Within a minute, the odors of methane and feces began drifting over the back rows. As the gas passed each row, kids began gagging and covering their noses with their shirts.

Moriah gave a deep stare at the other girls, who could tell her wheels were turning. It was a familiar look, for she was the science award winner of the class of 2018. She then began to explain diffusion movement of molecules. "Did you know that molecules move down a gradient of higher concentration to lower concentration? In this smelly scenario, Wally is the high concentration and we are the lower concentration. Our detection means our olfactory glands are receiving Wally's excrement. We are literally tasting his diarrhea."

Pam stated with a queasy expression, "Shut up, yah gonna make me puke!"

Laughing, Dalton said to no one in particular, "Durn it, Wally, that smells worse than my granddaddy's pig farm in July!" as Cherie called out, "Someone open a window!"Then, turning to her whole covey of friends, commanded, "Spray your perfume and get rid of that turdy smell!"

Meanwhile, Mr. King, the bus driver, turned slightly to say to Dr. Asbergski, (pronounced *"As-berger' ski"*) one of the chaperones and the supervising administrator on the senior trip to Florida, "Sir, could you please go see what the commotion is about back there?"

Asbergski began to make his way towards the rear when the invisible cloud of gastric gas reached his nose. "Agh! Did someone flatulate?" he gasped.

Dalton bellowed, "Dr. *Asperger*, no one farted. Wally just blew up the bus toilet!" Giggles echoed throughout the bus. Everyone called the vice-principal *Asperger* behind his back, but Dalton had no fear of incompetent authority figures, since at the age of eighteen, he already had his own landscape business and a large dump truck. At sixteen, Dalton had forged a fake CDL driver's license, and between fall and winter snowfalls and spring and summer grass cutting and landscaping, he was making close to $50,000 a year…and he always had managed to accumulate enough referrals by the middle of October so that his out-of-school suspensions would be served during deer season.

"Mr. Williams, I have told you time and time again that my name is Dr. Asbergski, pronounced " *As-berg'-ski.*" There was a rumor that he had the mild form of autism. Avoiding eye contact with anyone on the bus, he continued toward the back of the bus and stumbled on a seat mount, shaking his head and gritting his teeth, knowing that it was futile to try to control Dalton Williams. Laughter continued to echo throughout the bus. Red in the face, Asbergski snapped in a high-pitched whine as he attempted to open a window, "If you people can't behave in a respectful manner, I will call and have your parents come get you when we arrive!" Coach Buttito, standing behind Asbergski, looked at the students and rolled his eyes.

Amy Haddock, the captain of the cheerleaders, screamed out, "Open the windows!" In response, the bus driver got on the intercom to announce that the windows couldn't be opened, adding, "I have turned on the bus exhaust fans. All odors will be gone in two minutes."

Ignoring the bus driver's announcement, Asbergski shuffled, tripped on a backpack, and faltered back to the front of the bus to report to the driver, "Uh, they want to open the windows, okay?" The bus driver did not bother to respond, and simply rolled his eyes, sweeping his hand through his graying hair. Mumbling to himself, "How did this Dr. Asperger become an administrative role model for teenagers?! No wonder America's education is failing and our free society is on a slippery slope destined for anarchy."

Meanwhile, athletic director Butcher, awakened by the commotion and notorious for an annoying repetitive speech habit and baritone voice, shouted, "If the kids wanna open the windows, ya know whatta I mean, open the windows, you know what I mean? I used to teach third grade science and taught about the diffusion of molecules. If you open the windows, the gas odor can escape out the open windows, you know whatta I mean?" looking directly at Asbergski as she stroked her dark mustache.

Finally losing whatever patience he still retained, the seasoned driver exhaled loudly and then, with obvious frustration in his voice, repeated, "I said I turned the exhaust fans on. The odor will be gone in ninety seconds." Meanwhile, in the back, Wally was still producing.

Sensing the driver's irritation, Coach Buttito butted in, "What's goin' on in the back?"

"Wally's just usin' the bus's bathroom," Dalton informed him. "He's doin' number two and it's disgustingly fragrant, kinda like the county's sewage treatment plant." He and the kids in the front of the bus were now waving their hands in front of their faces.

Coach Buttito used this as a reason to go back by the girls, who were usually uncomfortable being around this coach and gym teacher with the large belly and habit of his eyes spending more time than necessary admiring their nubile teen bodies. There was a well-established rumor that he liked girl softball players especially, whose mothers were certain he coached third base to admire their tight softball pants.

Now done but hesitating in the bathroom, Wally was hoping desperately that the bus would stop before he had to walk down the narrow aisle. But after another five minutes, he knew it was time to make his way back to his seat. Leaving the dubious safety of the tiny lavatory, he shuffled swiftly with head down to avoid eye contact with anyone, slid into the vinyl seat, and slumped down in humiliation as he thought to himself, *"Why did I even come on this trip?"*

Chapter 2 Bus Attack

September 5, 2016 – 0800 HRS

The summer was over and the first day of school had arrived after a long hot summer in Greery, a small Colorado town. A light drizzle was falling, the droplets forming on the bus windows, making tiny rivers running down. The rain offered a welcome relief from the intense August heat that had descended for weeks on that part of the state. All the busses were in line at the reserved bus lot directly in front of Lincoln Elementary School. Most of the kids were wiping the bus windows, looking out with either the excitement of seeing friends again or the apprehension of what teacher was waiting for them. One little kindergartener, Jared, was especially anxious as he sat close to his big sister, Elizabeth, who couldn't offer the same feeling of comfort that his mother would have. Waiting at the front of the school were the teachers in the time-honored tradition of welcoming the children on the first day. As each bus entered the lot and took its place in line, the entire staff greeted them with a cheesy smile and waves. As the little pupils peeped through the windows at them, veteran teachers began some whispered and sarcastic remarks.

"Well, there's the menace!" burnt-out, middle-aged, fourth-grade teacher, Ms. Delaney, whispered into the ear of a young, fifth-grade teacher fresh out of Colorado State University.

"Are we ready to dump our loads?" the lead bus driver radioed to the twenty-five other yellow buses lined up behind him at the horseshoe-shaped bus drop, red lights flashing and the acrid odor of diesel exhaust growing stronger.

Bus 17 interrupted with "Negative, 85 is just now pulling in," the message reaching the rest of the drivers in the line.

As Jerry, driver of Number 85, set his emergency brake, he grabbed his mike. "Uh, sorry folks, that dang freight train had an extra boxcar and held me up on Syria Road. Well, anyway, here I am, ready to drop the restless rugrats."

"Jerry, you've been told: no slang on the radio!" the lead driver snapped, hearing the other drivers snicker because they were all familiar with Jerry's sense of humor.

"Ooops, sorry, I meant *the precious children*. Ya know what I mean," Jerry chuckled, his comments being heard by the entire county communications network. Finally, the lead driver gave the order, "Okay, roger that, 10-4, all busses open the doors and release the children."

As Taylor, the previously identified "menace" hopped down from his bus, he smiled devilishly and asked, "Hi, Ms. Delaney! Did you have a good summer? Then followed with a smirk and a wink, I'm real glad to see you again this year!"

"Yes, Taylor, I did," she answered with a fake smile, making the boy giggle, knowing full well that she hated him. She looked away from Taylor and rolled her brown eyes under her professionally plucked eyebrows. "Good luck with that one if he shows up on your class list," Delaney advised the new teacher. "His dad is an asshat, too, so you won't get any support from home. Taylor's the only child and a chip off the old block."

The giant analog clock over the school entrance struck 8:00 just as a blinding flash was followed by a deafening boom. Black smoke began rushing from Bus 85. An invisible compression wave reached the other busses; windows shattered and splinters of glass shredded the faces and bodies of children and the waiting teachers. The smaller children already off the busses were knocked down to the pavement by the shockwave.

Those who could still hear detected frightened voices screaming and echoing from the crowd, "85 just blew up!" "Fire!" An adult male voice bellowed, "Somebody call 9-11! Get 'em off the bus!"

"Oh, my God, 85's in flames!" cried out Coach Lindsey, the only female gym teacher. "Grab the kids! Get 'em outta here!" she screamed at the crowd, although most couldn't hear anything. The muscular teacher dashed into the flaming bus, grabbed four children, rushed them to safety behind the school sign, and then returned to the burning bus.

Elizabeth, a fourth-grader, screamed, "Please, Miss Lindsey, my little brother's still in there!"

Lindsey peered through the billowing black smoke and spotted a small figure, his clothes on fire, screaming, "Help! Help meee!" Dashing to the small child and gasping for air, she scooped him up and squeezed his little frame to her chest. Wrapping her well-built arms around him, she pressed his chest against her wet rain jacket, smothering the flames as she stumbled out of the smoking bus, choking, to place him gently on the ground. In her commanding voice, she cried, "Roll! Roll!" Several other teachers dashed up, rolling his small body in the wet grass until the flames were gone. His sister, terror-stricken, screamed, "JC, are you okay!?"

Although close to going into shock, the little boy moaned, "I think so." Lindsey's quickness had prevented the child from getting burns on his face. As Elizabeth began pulling his blackened shirt off, the little boy held up his hands, revealing slight burns on several fingers.

"Get him inside to the nurse!" a male adult voice ordered from somewhere in the chaos. Meanwhile, other children were still jumping out of the emergency exits, some with their backpacks smoking. Orange flames and rolling smoke poured from black holes that had once contained windows. The scene was hellish.

Within minutes, all the children had been pulled off Bus 85, but not all were alive. Nothing could stop the bus from burning; around it on the wet morning grass lay thrashing and lifeless bodies. The odor of burned flesh and rubber was unbearable. The burst tires, covered with flames, were searing themselves into the asphalt.

All individuals not injured by the blast huddled near the front entrance in total terror and shock when a second bomb, strategically placed in a trash can next to the front double doors, exploded. The sudden blast sent bodies into the air. Meanwhile, the sheriff's deputy, who had been on traffic duty out on the main highway, had been quick to evaluate the scene and had called for backup and medical help.

"Oh my God, we got two bombs that have exploded: one on a bus and the other one somewhere by the front entrance. We need immediate medical support…multiple ambulances, helicopters and the fire department. We need all available emergency personnel. Medical emergency. Medical emergency. Call all available rescue squads! Some bodies with injuries from nails and glass. It was an attack! My God, kids are dead. Innocent kids!"

The only thing the deputy couldn't report was who was responsible for launching a horrific attack on innocent children.

Chapter 3 Death to America

September 6, 2016 - 1000 HRS

Jama'at allkhwan al-Muslimin, the Muslim Brotherhood leaders, assembled around the long and narrow mahogany table. As the commander, Quibt, glared at each member, they began to fear his next words. Quibt's glaring and fanatical brown eyes focused on one particular man at the far corner of the large table. Quibt got up from his seat and walked towards the surprised subordinate. Putting cold hands on the apprehensive militant's shoulders, Quibt said, "Ahmad, you're a good man. You've been faithful to the movement." The subordinate relaxed and his shoulders drew back with pride. Heads nodded around the table. Slowly, Quibt took his right hand off one shoulder, and finding a long knife under his black thawb, he slipped the knife from its leather sheath. Light flashed off the polished steel blade as he reached around and stuck the knife into his unsuspecting victim's eye socket and flipped his eye onto the table. The victim screamed in pain as the bloody eye was rolling on the table. "Allah! Quibt, have mercy on me!" he screamed again, holding his hands over the empty orbital socket as blood seeped through his fingers.

The other terrorists sat stunned, in fear...except two senior militants who wore sadistic sneers. "I knew he was a spy!" growled one. "Can we torture the traitor before we behead him?"

Quibt informed his followers, "That's a false eye that stores a micro-camera. This American spy has recorded our every move and communicated our plans to the CIA for the last six months. Now it's time to use him!" Quibt said, speaking directly to the blood-wet eye that he now held in this hand as top military leaders thousands of miles away in the Pentagon were viewing it all on a large screen. He continued, "Jama'at allkhwan al-Muslimin will rule. Caliphate will govern all Americans. Your cities will experience our reign of terror like never before!"

Quibt turned the camera in the eyeball toward the still-screaming man. Another militant in a black hooded robe stood, holding a long curved knife; while grasping the spy's hair in one hand, in one quick swing, the henchman ended the man's screaming as his head fell to the table and blood splatter covered the camera lens.

Then Quibt claimed responsibility for a school bombing in Colorado.

"We blew up your children. We will continue to bring death to America. Your nation has only seen the beginning. Allah has given us the vision to judge and condemn the United States for their licentious lives. U.S. citizens are infidels and mutts of society. Every ethnic group on earth has immigrated to you. We have been given prophecy to cleans the world for only Islam. You no longer will be the world's most powerful nation. Allah will be the only holy one. The world will be governed and controlled by the caliphate. Islam will be the only religion. All other religions will be exterminated like insects. The brotherhood will conquer your way of life. America will be history. Western man shall die in unprecedented numbers and not by bombs alone. The death and destruction in your Old Testament will be but a triviality. The American women shall be ours. Each Islamic brother will have large harems. Your women will be our possessions and our slaves. America, the time is near when you will be facing unprecedented death." Quibt continued to glare at the camera, screaming, "Jihad! Jihad! Allah will rule the earth." With flecks of spit flying from between his fleshy lips, Quibt commanded,

"Draw back the curtain. Let the Americans see the power of Allah!"
A large black curtain was opened, revealing a majestic mosque filled
with men in dark robes, bowing in prayer as chorused chants to Allah
rang out.

"Rise up, my army!" shrieked Quibt. The remaining militants
around the table sprang to their feet, holding automatic weapons and
chanting, "JIHAD, JIHAD, JIHAD! Death to America!"

Chapter 4 Jungle Ride

April 16, 2018 - 1100 HRS

After picking their way through the hotel breakfast bar, the
students and chaperones traveled to their destination, Southern
Baptist Resurrection theme park. Even after being pushed by the
chaperones to arrive early, they soon discovered that the lines of
visitors waiting to get in stretched all the way back to the parking lot.
The sun was beating down on that 98-degree Florida day. With the
added humidity, caused by the Gulf of Mexico's warm water
evaporating and passing over central Florida, it made it feel degrees
hotter. Sweat poured off all of the kids and the adults. After a two-
hour wait in line, they finally entered the park.

Waiting in line for the rides was even worse, and as time
passed, the temperature continued to rise. Despite anxiously waiting
to experience the thrill of each main attraction, the excessive wait
and endless snaking around the enclosure chains became boring.
Walking back and forth for an average of ninety minutes did not
seem to get them any closer to each ride. At each attraction, they
would see the same people, the same kids fussing and crying, the
same lovers groping each other, and the same female classmates

experiencing the occasional uncomfortable appraisal from Coach Buttito.

With a frown, Ed declared, "These lines suck! They ought to pay us to do all this waiting!" showing his impatient frustration.

Wally replied, "Funny! We spent $125 a piece to wait in line for ninety-plus minutes for only a four-minute and thirty-second thrill."

After waiting in lines for several rides, Wally suggested, "Let's go to the Jungle Ride over there. It's shaded and we can go under the waterfall and get soaked to cool off."

Dalton said, "Hell, yeah, and let's position the girls so when we go under the waterfall, they'll get wet. I wanna see those...well, ya know."

With a big smile, "Man, you are brilliant!" Wally declared. "I'm gonna sit across from Cherie. Ed rolled his eyes, and reminded him, "Boy, after that doo doo you took, you ain't gotta even a chance!"

"Well, I'm not going," Mike said with a grunt. "I just bought these new Nikes and paid $150 for them." In response, Ed did not waver. "Well, I have serious swamp bottom and my underwear is stickin, so I'm goin' over there to the Jungle Ride."

With a shrug, Mike replied, "All right, I suppose my new kicks will dry in this heat. I'm game."

"Cool. Let's go, Mike," Wally said eagerly.

Dalton looked directly at Mike like some kind of commanding officer. "Mike, text Shelly. She likes you, so ask her to get the other hotties to come with us."

Minutes later at the Jungle Ride, Ed said with a whine, "Jeez, Louise, that guy said the wait here is still another ninety minutes from where we are! This is no better!"

"Come on, Ed! This is a little better. At least we're in the shade over here!" Mike muttered with forced enthusiasm, but he probably had plans to try grope Shelly a little while the others held their places in line.

Meanwhile, Wally was still undeterred and full of excitement about the ride, hopeful that Cherie was going to be with the other girls. Their part of the line was still in the shade with misting fans running full blast.

"Ed, let's you and me go get lunch and something cold to drink while they hold our place in line," Wally suggested.

Ed agreed, adding, "For a complete knucklehead, that's a good idea."

"I may be a knucklehead but you're a buttock, but I still consider you an honest good friend…." But before Ed and Wally could suggest picking up lunches and drinks for themselves and the other two, Mike exclaimed with lustful eyes, "Look, Shelly and the girls are finally coming!"

Wally, with a giant smile and hopeful eyes, observed, "Look, Cherie's in front. Thank God! I'm gonna marry that girl someday."

Mike rolled his eyes as if he knew absolutely everything about girls. "Boy, you don't have a chance! Well, maybe if you get a Corvette and become chief surgeon at the UVA Health Center."

Dalton, first to greet the girls, said, "Hey, Angela, how you doin'? You look a little hot and sweaty...but you always look hot," he added with a wink as his eyes slowly moved from her eyes, down to her little sandals, and back up again. As he finished his inspection, Angela gave him a look with her dark brown eyes that seemed to imply she had enjoyed the attention.

"Well, I *am* a little hot," she agreed.

Meanwhile, Cherie had been listening to Dalton's hapless attempt at charm but observing Wally. *"He's as excited as a ten-year-old,"* she thought. *"His boyish attitude makes me smile."* Cherie winked at him. Wally, surprised, smiled and turned away. *"He can't even hold eye contact with me. I think maybe he likes me. That's what I keep hearing, but he's too shy to say anything,"* she thought, letting out a sigh.

Finally, they reached their turn at the ride. Since the six of them did not fill an entire raft, a middle-aged couple wearing souvenir straw hats with miniature beer cans on the brims joined them to make eight occupants.

The man running the ride announced in a bored voice, sounding like a recording, *"Resurrection Theme Park strives to provide a safe environment for all patrons. Please abide by the following rules for your safety and the protection of our electronic equipment. You will get wet on this ride. The following rules are for your safety. Make sure all loose items are secured in the dry bags provided directly in front of you. Stay inside the raft at all times. Anyone pregnant or with heart conditions should not attempt this ride. Please remain seated and do not stand until we reach the end of the ride. Everyone ready?"*

After hearing the warnings, they were finally launched into their trip on a simulated Amazon River. The first thrill was a twenty-foot rubber alligator that suddenly appeared from beneath the surface and lunged toward the raft. The girls screamed while the boys were making their plans to position the boat so that the girls would get soaked in the rushing water of the now-approaching waterfall. Mike looked across the raft to Ed and Dalton with a huge grin, a grin that hadn't escaped the watchful gaze of Cherie. Then Wally pointed at the waterfall and gave the other two an equally huge wink. Cherie thought to herself, *"These guys are planning something. They're the kind my dad keeps warning me about -- total pigs and perverts!"*

Chapter 5   University of Virginia
The Ted Talk
November 19, 2015 - 1500 HRS

The introduction began: "Today we are going to hear from Dr. Arnold Benedict, chief researcher at Marshall University; Marshall might be considered a small university, but it's a big player in the field of gene manipulation. Dr. Benedict is renowned for his leading advances in agriculture and medicine. However, his most recent genetic findings have been applied to saving people from starvation and crippling bone cancer. Please give a warm welcome to Dr. Arnold Benedict."

Dr. Benedict stepped to the podium while the crowd clapped. He touched his nose and then stroked a rather scraggly goatee. With his right hand, he pinched the nosepiece of his wireless glasses, made an adjustment to the papers in front of him on the podium, and then began to address the audience.

"Thank you," he said in a strong voice that didn't match his slight frame contained in a somewhat rumpled brown suit. He bowed his head, more like a nod of humble appreciation.

"Thank you." In the silenced auditorium, each person seemed focused on the seventy-year-old. "Well, folks, I'm excited to share my ideas with you today. In the area of manipulated genetics, the possibilities are endless to make life better for every citizen in the United States and the world, especially still-developing countries faced with hunger and disease. We can now stop cancer. We can feed the growing world population. We can raise the standard of living in the poverty-stricken areas of the world. Yes, we can."

The crowd clapped for a long minute. He again nodded his head. "We will live in a new world. The genetic manipulation industry will advance faster than the cyber world. Mankind has never experienced such promising power. Today, I stand before you to present ideas that will change medicine and agriculture. Using the very fiber of a living system, we can stop cancer through genetic manipulation and we can feed millions that are presently without food and clean water."

Dr. Benedict paused, pushed his glasses higher on his nose, and stared out at the two thousand scientists and students that had come to hear him speak at the JPJ Convention Center on the University of Virginia campus. "Ya know, I'm a *Pirates of the Caribbean* fan. I think I've watched the series at least ten times. I'll bet many of you ladies like that Johnny Depp fellow." Some laughter rumbled through the audience. "Yes, ladies, that's what I thought," he observed with a wide grin. "Those films offer humorous versions of a very unruly time in our Colonial history. The pirates would sail across the seas, stealing booty. Those rascally villains never worked to find the treasures; they just took the products of somebody else's labors. My friends, in today's world, *viruses* are the pirates of cellular life, tiny beings that cannot produce offspring. Instead, viruses invade cells, or to adhere to the pirate analogy, they "board the cellular ship," and use the cell's genetic machinery to produce endless populations of cloned viruses. Millions of replicated viruses can be produced in hours. Even our fastest copiers cannot produce numbers like we are studying. Viruses have truly staggering reproductive systems. In other words, once a virus infiltrates the nuclear DNA, it can produce counterfeit proteins."

Benedict continued.

"These invasive creatures infiltrate and modify the human DNA, and we experience viral diseases: Ebola, chicken pox, flu, and of course, as we all have experienced, the common cold. Some of these illnesses are devastating while some are just plain old nuisances. Ebola and flu virus board our genome and wreak havoc on our bodily systems. I am certain that all of us are familiar with the symptoms, or our bodies' reactions to these metabolic attacks." Benedict adjusted his glasses again while reviewing his detailed lecture notes.

When he lectured, his voice made his listeners feel as if they were having a one-to-one conversation with a favorite uncle. He had a gleam in his eye that could not be faked; his entire body language announced his love for his subject matter. His demeanor was contagious, and those who shared a passion for the subject could not help but be enthused by his own passion and desire to lead technology in the advancements of agriculture and medicine. There was, however, one listener, a rather swarthy complexioned man, in a new but somewhat poorly fitting suit, who sat in the second row. In his jacket pocket, a small digital recorder was whirring silently.

"My friends, there is power beyond imagination in the living system. We, as biologists, cannot produce the primordial soup, but we can add some seasoning to it. The blueprints in the cell store information for every tiny little metabolic activity, such as identifying foreign cells and potentially damaging molecules, a thermostat-like regulation used to produce more energy when needed for work, and the recognition and replacement of fatigued organelles. It holds more information than the combined social services of New York City!"

He chuckled. "Some of you older folks may recognize that old advertising quote. The rest of you, the young brilliant scientists, can take my ideas and make a societal change for the better." Another smile appeared across his face. "In biological terms, The DNA controls machinery that makes biological molecules, proteins and signaling lipids. These biological compounds control digestion, waste removal, and ATP supply in the nano-world of metabolic sustainability. Man understands the mechanics of this tiny world, but the manipulation of using a programmed retrovirus is the core of my lecture today. Today, I will explain to you the how and why. Unfortunately, without my lab equipment, we will not produce an engineered protein today, but you *are* invited to come to see my team at work at Marshall University." Meanwhile, toward the rear of the lecture hall, two other men with dark complexions and suits identical to the one being worn by the individual in the second row, looked at each other. One whispered, "We must use that man and his knowledge for our cause!" receiving a warning frown from his companion. Benedict's commanding voice continued from the front.

"My first effort to harness this genetic force was in the fight against Type I diabetes. As I walked through UVA's CCU, I saw a child connected to tubes and pumps. The little fellow was bloated from all the fluids being forced into his underweight forty-pound body. I thought to myself, 'God, how can I relieve this child of the ball and chain of the insulin infusion?' Doing more research, I found that the pancreas simply does not produce the natural hormone for blood levels of glucose. The biological mechanism to control hyperglycemia was non-functional. So my team raised the question of how can we reprogram cells located in the Islets of Langerhans to produce functional insulin? Dr. Byrd, my mentor and my genetics professor at Marshall, suggested that we analyze the relative DNA and review patients' health records in the hopes that one of them may not suffer from the metabolic deficiency. Eventually, she found that a cousin of one patient, John Brian, was clear of all diabetes. We extracted his DNA and located pBR322 loci. This was the malfunctioning gene in Wesley, my patient. We knew the correct DNA sequence for perfect beta cells, using the power of the retrovirus to reprogram Wes's DNA and to produce the regulating organic compound. We shared our findings with the medical world and now children all over the planet are rid of the complications of Diabetes I!"

Two med students from UVA stood and began to clap, followed by the entire audience who rose to their feet, still viewing the slide show on the big screen, which showed Wes, wearing his football uniform with number 22. Dr. Benedict flashed another ear-to-ear smile. "That little forty-pound boy now weighs 177 and is an All-American halfback. When I get a chance, I sit with his parents in the Marshall stands on Friday nights and celebrate Wes running the football." This revelation was met with more applause.

"This genetic manipulation is not limited to humans," Benedict continued after the applause faded and all were seated. "Years ago, in my young past, I was slightly brainwashed by an egocentric Pentecostal preacher who was more interested in constructing a giant temple in central America than in bringing people to Jesus Christ. Anyway, getting back to the point, back then, I was among a group of this preacher's teenage followers on a mission to Honduras. This trip is forever in my memory and majorly influenced how I view life in the United States.

"One of our mission's goals on the trip was to provide village children nutritious meals at the village food hall. Even at my young age, the experience shamed me and opened my eyes to wasteful habits regarding food here in the U.S. Every noon, these children silently packed a twelve-by-twelve room and sat patiently, waiting for their daily nourishment. Then and there, I wanted to make a difference in the lives of these deprived children. These innocent and malnourished children needed help; some were already orphaned by the early deaths of parents. I realized that a bowl of rice was not enough to sustain these kids and provide all essential proteins.

Legumes full of protein were missing from their diets. Recently, my team again went to the labs and studied the harsh environment of tropical and subtropical dry forests. We extracted a gene from the columnar cactus and now, through gene manipulation, legumes grow all over the steep mountainsides of the Honduran landscape. In one season, we supplied villagers with pounds and pounds of that vital protein supplement. More children are attending school and their general health has improved. Folks, one plant and one gene saved an entire people from debilitating health problems and possible eventual starvation!"

The scientists and students in the audience again stood for a three-minute ovation…while the two men in the rear stood as well, nodding at each other.

Chapter 6 Bat Blood: Florida

April 16, 2018 – 2200 HRS

"Let's go!" Dalton said in a commanding low whisper, as if he were preparing his troops to infiltrate a combat zone behind enemy lines.

Mike, startled by his command, asked, "Where are we going with such a short notice?"

Ed offered, "Who cares? It's gotta be better than sitting in this hotel!"

The three slipped quietly down the fire escape from the sixth floor, exiting the hotel building and stepping onto the asphalt of the darkened rear parking lot. "Let's go this way," directed Dalton, pointing down a shrub-bordered path and through a cut hole in a chain-link fence. Through the gaping hole, they saw a silhouetted house. As the boys crept closer to what was a vacant building, Mike realized it was a decades-old theater. The name on the marquee, in faded letters, was *Hebron Theater*. In the early years of the Southern Baptist Resurrection amusement park, this old facility had staged all sorts of Christian dramas and musicals and had been the birthplace of contemporary Christian rock music. The new modern theater, **Zemke's Playhouse,** had replaced the aging building to accommodate contemporary light shows and special effects performed at the amusement park. The boys slid through a badly weathered and cracked rear stage door, off its hinges, making for an easy entrance.

The aging structure was pitch black inside, making it nearly impossible to navigate; the only thing detectable were their shortened steps as Dalton, Mike and Ed shuffled their feet and held their hands out in front, feeling their path through musty curtains and ropes. After stumbling over and into old theatrical props and dodging cobwebs, they made their way to a small room at the back wall of the stage.

Not paying attention to Ed, Mike's nose collided with the back of Ed's head. "Ouch, what did you stop for? "Mike grunted, wiping eyes that were watery as he rubbed his nose.

Ed whispered, "I think this is the dressing room."

Dalton turned his cell phone light on, checking himself in a dusty mirror. Glancing down, he spotted a very large black trunk.

Ed reached down, and, lifting the trunk's lid, said, "Hey, let's see what's inside? Bring that light over here." A large plume of dust rose in the air. The boys waved their hand to see through the musty air. "Ooooh, I hate that mildew smell!" Ed whined.

Dalton shined his cell phone light inside the trunk. As Mike peered over Dalton's shoulder to see what treasures might be in the trunk, a bat flew down from somewhere in the darkness and tried to land in Mike's curly hair. Mike screamed, "Help git it out, it's in my hair! It's gettin' tangled!" he shouted, flailing his arms in the air. Meanwhile, the bat was doing its own kind of shrieking and making clipping noises.

Dalton started to laugh. "It's just a little old bat. I'll get it out." He reached to grab the bat and the bat bit him, puncturing the fleshy spot on Dalton's hand. "Ouch, I'm bleeding!" Dalton moaned, no longer laughing.

Ed picked up a white cane, some leftover prop on the stage, and began swinging it, striking the bat, and seemingly stunning it. Mike pulled the bat from his hair as bat blood dripped down his face and threw it onto the floor.

Dalton said, "Let's go before Coach Buttito knows we're gone. I've gotta wash this hand! It might give me a disease and we have only ten minutes to get back in our rooms before the big Buttito returns from the Gentlemen's Club down the street."

Scrambling back up to the sixth floor, the three jumped into bed with their shoes and pants still on just as Coach Buttito banged on the door.

Ed slowly cracked open the door and peeked out. "Hey, Coach, we're all here and accounted for."

"Good, because if Dalton is not, I'm going to find 'im and choke 'im."

"Hey, Buttito, here I am in bed, see? Please tell me a story and tuck me in. Ya know, maybe something about one of those pole dancers at the Gentlemen's Club."

"Shut up, you little degenerate!" grunted Buttito, looking over Ed's shoulder through the door.

Ed snickered, covering his mouth with a fist as Mike put his head on his pillow and laughing loudly enough to wake Wally, who had been asleep.

Wally grumbled, "Turn off the light, you guys! I'm having a good dream!"

"Durn it, Wally, I have to share that bed with you. Your dream better not be a wet one!" Mike snapped as Ed closed the door and slid the chain lock closed.

"Hey, Dalton, why did we take these musty old costumes from that trunk?" Ed asked.

"You wait; I've got a plan an' you're gonna love it!"

Chapter 7   Charlottesville

November 19, 2015 - 1700 HRS

Benedict spent a few minutes after his lecture to answer some questions from individuals, but a quick glance at his watch told him he needed to leave in order to get back to Marshall ahead of rush-hour traffic. Offering apologies for having to leave other questions unanswered, he jogged down the concrete steps of the academic building, hoping he remembered correctly where he had parked his Toyota Prius.

"Lot C, I think," he muttered to himself as he scanned the signs atop various light posts, and sure enough, he saw his car as he entered the second row of parking spaces.

Pushing the button on his remote, he could see his tail lights flash in answer to the remote. Just as he opened the driver's side door, hands gripped both his arms and a heavily accented voice whispered softly but sinisterly in his ear.

"Do nothing stupid, Doctor Benedict!" the voice commanded as a white van, or what had been white before accumulating what looked to be the entire winter's road dirt, rushed up, the side door sliding open before the van had even come to a complete stop. The two men that held Benedict pushed him roughly into the open space as another man inside pulled him in by the lapels on his suit jacket and held him to the metal floor, his knees grinding into Benedict's back as he searched his pockets. In no more than a minute's passage, Benedict found himself with a coarse cloth bag over his head while he was bound by plastic strips, his arms behind him. Someone reached under the bag and quickly stuffed something dry and soft into his mouth, followed by a wide strip of duct tape, although Benedict couldn't see for sure. During the whole operation, nothing was said among the kidnappers, the van's motor the only sound besides the grunting of the scientist as he struggled, to no avail, against his attackers. In not more than a minute, the van door was slammed shut and the vehicle was moving.

"Slow down!" a different voice commanded the driver. "We do not want to draw attention!"

Benedict heard that command was answered with a grunt, presumably from the driver. Within another five minutes, Benedict could tell that they had finished maneuvering through Charlottesville's city streets and were on the interstate, the rapidly accelerating van pushing Benedict back against the stiff, cold seat.

He was trying to listen for any outside sounds that might indicate where they were, or in what direction they were traveling when he felt a sharp prick in his right bicep. He was trying to push out the wad of cloth in his mouth when he lost consciousness.

Benedict had no idea where he was or how long he had been unconscious, but he had no doubt that at some time, they had traded the dirty white van for an airplane; there was no mistaking the steady drone of jet engines. Shaking his head to try to remove the cobwebs of whatever drug he had been injected with, the bag over his head was abruptly yanked off. Blinking rapidly at the sudden brightness, he saw a middle-aged man in a gray silk suit, a full beard framing a dark complexion, in the seat next to him. There was also no mistaking the glaring dark eyes that were attempting to bore into his own.

"Well, I trust you have had a nice nap, Doctor. You will need the rest for the journey ahead."

It was then that Benedict became aware that not only was he in a small private jet and securely held in place with a seat belt, but there was also a webbed belt of some kind tightly secured across his chest, fastened to the back of his soft leather seat. He could move nothing but his legs and head.

Coughing several times and trying to find some saliva in a very dry mouth, he was able to ask where he was, though in a croaking voice.

"You are on a very important journey, Doctor," the man replied. "You are going to be instrumental in assisting us with our divine mission!"

"And what may that be?" Benedict asked sarcastically, "And who are you?" intensifying his tone.

"Of course you may ask," his companion responded with some sarcasm as well. "I am Quibt, a humble soldier in the army of Allah."

"That suit you're wearing must've cost three hundred bucks, so I doubt you're very humble," Benedict growled.

"Actually, closer to four hundred pounds in London a week ago, but never mind that. You are on your way to assisting a fellow scientist in the creation of a genetically manipulated virus."

"To help mankind in the name of Allah, no doubt!" Benedict snapped.

Quibt laughed. "Oh, yes. Well, to help a specific portion of mankind, at least. Would you like some water?"

Somewhat startled by the change of topic, Benedict nodded, hoping that the water would not contain more drugs. One of Quibt's men, who suddenly appeared in the aisle where Benedict could see him, held out a bottle of Poland Spring water. Taking it from the man, Quibt twisted the cap. The plastic snap of a newly opened bottle was unmistakable, removing Benedict's concern about the water.

Quibt held the bottle to Benedict's lips.

"What, no straw?" Benedict muttered.

"Sorry," Quibt said, not sounding at all sorry. "If you're careful, you won't get any water on your American Men's Wearhouse suit. Yes, I've seen the commercials, Doctor."

Thoughts of all kinds had been racing through the scientist's mind.

"How do you expect me to cooperate with you in whatever scheme you plan, if I may ask the obvious question," Benedict practically spat, making eye contact with the fanatic's dark shifting eyes. "Have you considered that when they discover my unlocked car sitting alone in that huge parking lot, they will realize that something bad has happened to me?"

Quibt smiled. "Alas, your car is no longer sitting in that huge parking lot. You may remember one of my men going through your pockets. That car is on its way to some rural road in Virginia heading to the bottom of the James River. No one knows anything but what they believe, that you are on your way back to West Virginia and Marshall University."

"*They know all about me*," Benedict thought as his hopes began to fade for a speedy rescue from what he could only assume were some sect of Islamic terrorists.

"And we have no doubt that you will want to be completely cooperative with us…so nothing bad happens to that lovely blond daughter living in Partridge Hall at Bowdoin College there in Maine."

Chapter 8   Florida: Prospect Rock Restaurant

April 17, 2018 - 1700 HRS

The Sherman Shifflett Memorial High School graduating class of 2018 sat waiting for the pre-ordered dinner at the Prospect Rock Restaurant. Instruments, eight-by-ten, black-and-white photographs of great rock musicians, and famous concert murals decorated the walls. The ambience and theme were almost tangible: great American rock music. The restaurant was known for its launching of young rockers and pop singers. More than a few kids in the past had met with almost instant stardom performing at this moderately priced eatery in the touristy town of Tabel, Florida, named for a famous shrimp fisherman and his family. The restaurant was a special stop on the senior field trip; many of the high-school musicians were thrilled to get their chance to perform in front of a live audience.

"Dr. Asbergski, what is this instrument?" asked Wally, pointing to a large, eight-stringed instrument on the wall above their booth.

"Well, I used to teach Earth Science," Asbergski (still pronounced Asperger) replied. Wally and Mike raised their eyebrows and waited for a more relevant answer. "I spent the summer of '97 taking a class at Virginia Tech on sedimentary rock superposition," Asbergski (still pronounced Asperger) added with a nod and a smile.

"Uh, that's great," muttered Ed. looking as puzzled as the others, his face reflecting his thoughts of *"what does Earth Science have to do with these eight strings on a wooden board?"* Asbergski continued, "Well, my favorite restaurant had bluegrass every Wednesday night and some Blue Ridge hillbilly would play the mountain folk music and he called something that looked like this his harp."

Meanwhile, while Asbergski was getting deeper into his lecture, Dalton switched Mentiroso's room key with the assistant principal's that was sitting on the tabletop. No one else seemed to notice the exchange…no one except Mike, that is, who cocked his head slightly, eyebrows raised.

"Durn it, we've waited for an hour and ten minutes to eat a lousy Stouffer's barbequed chicken dinner?! How much did we pay for this?" Mike grumbled.

At that moment, Wally announced, "Hey! Open mike is gonna start!"

Their cardboard dinners momentarily forgotten, the students turned their attention to the small but brightly lit stage.

Of their group, the first brave soul was Ginny Perkins, an All-State soprano who did a passable job of Aretha Franklin's "R-E-S-P-E-C-T." The crowd of students and the few locals clapped, seemingly impressed with the talent of the young brunette.

"Well, she's overweight enough an' got a good voice like Aretha, though she's white, but I gotta admit, she's pretty good," Dalton whispered to Mike.

"Yeah, she's got a great voice," Mike whispered back.

The emcee stepped onto the stage and announced, "Well, little lady, you just rocked my world! Wanna see me after the show?"

"No!" replied Ginny assertively, making her way back to her table amid some laughter from the audience.

"Well, who's next?" the emcee asked, looking around the large room.

Mike looked directly at Wally. "Go, buddy, get a guitar and play! Show'em your talent and God's gift to rock 'n' roll!"

Wally, shying away from the moment of opportunity, looked away to avoid eye contact. "No, I'm not good enough yet," he argued softly.

Ed looked directly into Wally's eyes and said, "Boy, you are oneheckuva good guitar player an' you've been strummin' and pickin' at that thing since you were thirteen. Get your ass on stage an' show Perkins who's the best!"

Ed's encouragement came from the fact that he had finally beaten Ginny Perkins for class president, and whenever he got a chance, he would take the opportunity to show her up. Ginny had beaten Ed in every class election since seventh grade until Ed had finally won at the end of their junior year.

Dalton piped in, "Wally, get your ass on stage. Whateryaa scared of – doo doo'n' your pants up there?"

"Dalton, why'd you have to say *that*?" Wally grumbled, shaking his head as Ed laughed and slapped Wally on the back of his head.

Ignoring Ed's and Dalton's intentions, Mike showed some kindness for once and tried to express his confidence in Wally. "Wally, I believe in you, so get some confidence and jump up on stage! You can do this. Show them who's the best."

Letting out a long sigh, Wally said, "Okay, Mike, I'll do it!" Sliding out of the booth, he sprang up on stage with newfound sureness and grabbed a house Gibson. Plugging the borrowed guitar into an amp, Wally stepped up to the microphone, tried a few chords, and then began in rhythmic precision, playing the first few chords to Zeppelin's "Stairway to Heaven." The emcee stepped back off the stage as heads turned to watch and listen to this unlikely guitar master. The lighting on the stage dimmed with a single spot shining directly on Wally. At that moment, Wally realized, *"This is my chance! These folks ain't heard nothing yet!"* He stopped momentarily, smiled, pulled the mike close to his lips with calm, confident coolness. He played a riff that no one had ever heard before, one that he had created in the private solitude of his bedroom. Suddenly, it occurred to many of his classmates that Wally's stage presence was unlike his usual introverted persona. Ginny Perkins's mouth dropped open as Wally looked out at the audience, gave a quick wink at Cherie, and began.

"You may drive around the town
In a brand new shiny car
Your face in the wind and your haircut's in
And your friends think you're bizarre

You may find a cushy job and I hope that you go far
But if you really want to taste some cool success
You better learn to play guitar

Play guitar, play guitar
Play guitar, oh yeah
[x2]

You got your eyes on the cheerleader queen
You're walkin' her home from school
You know that she's only seventeen
But you know she's gonna make you a fool

You know you can't touch that stuff
Without money or a brand new car
Let me give you some good advice, young man
You better learn to play guitar

Play guitar, play guitar
Play guitar, oh yeah
[x2]

You may think all women around the world want a phony rock star
But you're wrong,

They want a guy who plays guitar"

(Lyrics by John Melancamp)

Then Wally launched into a two-minute guitar solo that would have rivaled anything Jimmy Page could have produced with just six strings and no special audio effects. While the rest were still enthralled by this high school student's surprising talent, Dalton looked around at "the posse," and whispered, "Psst! This is our chance!"

The small crowd of his classmates began to stand, astonished, as some began to turn on their cell phone lights. Wally finished and gently put the borrowed Gibson back, while the audience shouted, "More! Encore, encore!" Wally started walking off stage as Dalton screamed out, "Wally! Wally!" with Mike and Ed…and Cherie, her eyes and mouth wide open, echoing the same. Soon the full house was chanting Wally's name, even the local customers who didn't even know him.

Coach Buttito looked across the table of chaperones at the athletic director Butcher and rolled his eyes. "My God, of all people, that goofy Wally kid?! I still wanna choke that kid for the toilet incident! He stunk up the entire bus. What a goof ball!"

Asberski, briefly taking his eyes off the stage, remarked, "Yeah, his doo doo stinks, but you got to admit, that kid can play."

Butcher, with a head nod, said, "Asberski, I have to agree with you there."

Meanwhile, the rest of the restaurant watched Wally return to the small stage and play two more songs: "Take It Easy" by The Eagles and the other a Bob Seger classic.

As the adults were discussing Wally's performance and focused on the music, the perve posse quietly sneaked out the back door of the restaurant, unnoticed.

Mike looked at Ed, "Where are we goin?"

"You'll see," was all Ed was willing to say.

Chapter 9 Undercover Undergarments

April 18, 2018 - 2200 HRS

The boys left the Prospect Rock Restaurant, ran across the connected parking lot to their hotel, slipped through the lobby, and dashed directly to the back staircase. Speeding up the steps, they opened the fire escape door on the fourth floor.

"This is the floor," Dalton gasped, trying to catch his breath. "We'll dress here in the custodian's closet!" They grabbed the Old Testament costumes that they had stashed there on the fourth floor before they left for dinner. Dalton grabbed the Pharaoh get-up.

Ed whined, "Why do you get to be Pharaoh? I want to be the Pharaoh!"

"Aw, shut up, Ed," Dalton snapped, "you can be Moses or Aaron…or any of the others. They must've performed *The Ten Commandments* for years in this old, musty theater…. even without Charlton Heston!"

"It doesn't matter!" Mike grunted, pulling at some kind of headdress, "Get one of these wigs and wrap a loin cloth around your waist, and hurry! Wally only knows ten songs an' none of them are long. Hopefully, somebody else will play or sing! Buttito will kill us if he realizes we're missing!"

"Aah, don't worry, Mike, he's sure to go to the restaurant bar and add to his fat beer belly!" Dalton giggled, dressed in full Pharaoh outfit. Standing in front of a filmy mirror, covered with closet dust, he posed, head and chin held high as he bounced the gold-painted scepter on the floor. Mike, dressed as Aaron, put on the long gray wig and beard, almost completely covering his face, while Ed, as Moses, was completely covered; no one could identify any of them, they were sure. The fake goat skin skirt was short and wrapped around Ed's upper thighs. "Man, I hope my ding dong doesn't slip below my skirt line!"

"You still believe you have a big one, huh? Dream on, my boy," Mike said with a chuckle.

"Well, mine's still larger than yours!" boasted Ed.

"Okay, you guys," Dalton announced. "I have the key. The girls are in room 609 an' we gotta hurry. Just remember to keep your back to the security camera in the hall."

Outside the girls' room, Dalton slipped the card into the magnetic lock. The green light flashed as Dalton pushed open the door. "Find all the bikini tops, swimsuits and sports bras! Throw the stuff into this pillowcase."

The girls' bags were all over the room, making finding everything difficult. Some clothes were on the floor, some still in suitcases, and even more in dresser drawers. Dalton exclaimed, "Make sure we have everything. Check the suitcases. Mike, Ed, get all the stuff on the floor. I'll get the stuff hanging in the shower. Don't miss anything!"

Mike questioned, "Is this like a panty raid? Take them, too?"

"No, just whatever will cover the top half," Dalton replied with a grin.

"Why?" Ed asked completely puzzled.

"Oh, let's just say the day at the pool is going to be exciting in many ways," Dalton semi-explained, trying to be mysterious.

"Durn it, this fake hair is making me hot! I'm sweating and it's starting to drip into my eyes!" Mike grumbled as he wiped the sweat with his forearm, stuffing bras into the pillowcase.

Dalton ordered, "Get that stuff in Kelly's suitcase and let's hurry. We only got a few minutes before the show is over."

"I have everything," said Mike.

"Me, too," Ed acknowledged

"Okay, let's get outta here," ordered Dalton in a whisper, opening the door and peeking out. "An' don't forget the security camera in the hall!"

"Where we gonna hide the pillowcases?" Ed asked as they ran down the hallway.

Skidding to a stop in front of a door, Dalton whispered, "This is it, room 613." We'll put them under Asperger's and Butthead's beds," Dalton instructed. Mike began to laugh as they opened the chaperones' door.

The boys stuffed the pillowcases under the two beds and pulled the bedspreads up so that the pillowcases weren't visible. They ran out of the room, keeping their backs to the camera. "Let's ditch the costumes in Mentiroso's room," Dalton suggested. Ed snickered and put his fist over his mouth. "No matter what he says, no one is going to believe that liar. He cheated his way to number two in the class until the Biology 101 teacher caught him cheating on the first two exams. They'll think it was him and his two prep boys from the golf team. Meanwhile, we'll be in the clear 'cause everyone knows they'll try to lie their way out of it and they won't believe a word they say, not after the time they got caught cheating at the district golf match."

"Good idea, Ed," Mike said with a smile.

Having left the costumes in their classmate's room, Dalton peeked back out in the hallway.

"Okay, coast is clear," said Dalton, "Hurry up! We gotta get back to the restaurant."

Sneaking through the rear kitchen door and slipping past the two chefs who were busy with food preparation, the boys made their way to the table. As they sat down, Mike grinned. "We actually pulled it off!" he whispered conspiratorially.

Ed, still confused, asked, "Dalton, why did we just take the bras and tops?"

With a smirk, Dalton winked and said, "You'll see, my boy, you'll see!"

Chapter 10 Your Choice

November 20, 2015 - 0800 HRS

Melik, one of Quibt's top terrorists, invited Benedict to sit on the soft, brown-leather couch and offered him a glass of *Maker's Mark,* holding the full bottle up.

"I have heard you like the best of all pleasures. Would you like it with ice -- I believe you Americans call it "on the rocks" -- or neat, as the Brits called it when I was at Cambridge?" Melik asked.

Surprised by the presence of strong bourbon, Benedict replied, "Well, after a week of a total absence of such generous hospitality, I guess I could use a drink. Straight...um, neat. Without being rude to my gracious 'host,' I have no idea who you are and what you represent. Most likely, you have nothing that I want or need...and even more likely, I doubt that I have anything for you. So what do I have to do to get back home?"

Melik grimaced a little. "Dr. Benedict, you are known to be a good man and I know you want to help good people. Let me assure you, we have the best of intentions."

"That's interesting," Benedict said, accepting the glass of bourbon, "but I do not see it that way, considering that you threw me into a van and kept me in a kennel for a week. I believe that's called kidnapping here *and* in England *and* wherever you are from, and if I'm not badly mistaken, you are still holding me hostage!"

"Ah, Dr. Benedict, that was for your own good," Melik murmured smoothly.

"What!?"

"You can now be treated like a king or a slave. The choice is yours!" Benedict's host replied with a slight smirk.

Taking a sip and wishing he was in Kentucky instead of wherever he was, Benedict snapped, "What do you want from me? Get to the point!"

Sitting back in an overstuffed armchair, Khayyam explained, "Our enemies have defiled our culture and they have captured and murdered our women and children. Military force and bombs are not stopping the enemy from these crimes. We want to remove them from the planet. Once the evil ones are removed, our peaceful people can have an opportunity for education in the old ways. Dr. Benedict, you can help us preserve our culture – our beliefs and way of life. That is why you are here."

Leaning forward and glaring, Benedict growled, "I have never heard genocide put so gently before. My research and knowledge will never be used for evil and war…and if they are parts of your so-called culture, you will never receive any help from me!"

Seeming to ignore the scientist's anger, the Arab replied, "Dr. Benedict, we simply want you to teach us how to program a virus. You call it retroviral engineering. Your knowledge can help our people to regain the life we deserve. It has been taken from us and we are going to get it back. It is that simple."

"Really? That simple? You have no idea of the power genetic manipulation can have on a population, especially on a human population. A simple mistake by a few can lead to complete devastation to all. No. I believe that is as simple as it gets."

Melik shook his head. "You will share with us your technology to modify a cell by genetic manipulation or….. well, let's just say you will be more than willing to offer your assistance. For your assistance, we are offering you six million dollars that will be placed in an offshore account of your choosing. I would think that would give your research and lab facilities a boost. Or you can endure various tortures…of our choosing. But again, that choice is totally yours."

"I refuse to consider it. No. I will not share my research with you bastards, whoever you are or claim to be!"

Melik sprang to his feet, his smooth smile replaced by a rigid snarl. "Fine!" Turning toward the closed door, he shouted, "Guards, take this American infidel back to the cell. This time, no food or water and strip him of the fine clothes he is wearing! Temperature forty degrees!" Melik snapped as two, thick-necked men entered and hustled Benedict from the room, their fingers digging into his biceps.

Twenty-four hours passed, by which time Benedict's lips had turned purple, his whole body shaking as he lay curled in the fetal position. Then the same metal door was thrown open as Melik and the two guards entered, one wheeling in a tall cart on which sat a television monitor and a VCR.

As Benedict sat up, still unable to halt his body's tremors, Melik commanded the guard, "Plug them in and turn them on!"

As the screen slowly lit up, it showed a video of the front of a house, as if taken from the street. Melik asked, "Dr. Benedict, do you recognize this house?"

He did not respond, but Benedict knew the residence: it was the home of his best friend, Dr. Bill Daily, a physicist and old college buddy who now worked for Grumman Corporation. College fraternity brothers, they still mountain biked together.

"Now, Dr. Benedict, we come to a new choice, and the choice is yours... the choice is Mr. Daily lives or dies. I have a sniper in a rented house across the street from that house. He is only forty yards from the target. He will not miss. We have been watching him for days and know that your old friend Bill sits in his office every night at nine o'clock. His desk is positioned at the window. Again, my shooter will not miss. With a simple phone call, on my command, he will fire two rounds, one in the forehead and the other behind his right ear. The choice is yours. Will you assist my scientists? If you say yes, the money will double and you will be set free upon the evidence that the engineered virus eradicates our enemies. Well, Dr. Arnold Benedict, what is your choice – be rich or join your friend Bill in death?"

Chapter 11 At the Pool

April 17, 2018 – 1000 HRS

Cherie stepped out of the shower, dried off, and began to dress for the free day at the pool. Excited to put on her leopard-skin bikini for the first time, she rummaged through her small suitcase to find only the bottoms.

" Oh, no, how did I forget the bikini top?!" she moaned, shocked because the new bathing suit was the first thing she remembered packing for the trip.

"What's wrong?" asked Stacy and Angela at the exact same time, coming back into their room and seeing the dismayed look on Cherie's face.

"I don't have my bikini top!" Cherie told them in a disgruntled tone, her hands on her naked hips.

"Are you sure you packed it?" asked Angela.

"Yeah, I am. Mom and I argued that the suit was too revealing. I'll just have to wear my black suit from last year. I brought it just in case we were going to swim in the ocean 'cause the label on my new one says that salt water can have a fading effect on the dyes in the fabric," she explained as she continued to search frantically through the small suitcase, as if more searching would make the top appear.

"What the heck? The top to the black one is missing, too…and all my bras are missing! What the heck?!"

Angela, Stacy, and Kelly all dashed to look into their own luggage.

Kelly was first to report: "My stuff is gone, too. Bikini top and all my sports bras. The only thing I have is the trip T-shirt. The last thing I want to wear is that stupid shirt. I never liked the design from the beginning. More importantly, I don't want any guys to know that I'm still in high school!"

Angela cried out, "That's all that's left in my luggage, too!"

Kelly, with an angry frown, blurted, "Dalton and his perv posse! I bet that's the durn answer!"

"But how?" asked Cherie.

Angela, her face already flushed, snapped, "I don't know how or when, but I bet Kelly's right. Dalton and the perves."

"Well, I'm not gonna give that redneck or his friends the satisfaction of getting angry and accusing him. I'm putting on the stupid senior-class T-shirt and heading to the pool as if nothing is missing. At least they'll be confused and disappointed that their raid accomplished nothing and they'll get no pleasure from their perverted adventure. They're gettin' no reaction from me, those durn perverts!" Kelly growled, her jaw clenched tightly. The others grunted in agreement.

Arriving at the pool, Angela and Stacy did their best to ignore the boys sitting in chairs surrounding a little Tiki hut where the resort had piled complimentary towels and other assorted amenities for guests. Dalton had gone ahead and purchased a bottle of tanning oil with the resort's logo on it, not because he was interested in solar protection, but because the purchase came with a complimentary massage and oil application by some nubile female employees at the pool. Indeed, two beautiful, golden-skinned brunettes were already rubbing tanning oil on Mike's and Ed's shoulders, the girls' perfect bodies highlighted in matching bright yellow bikinis that covered very little.

Wally, dazzled by the attention that his two buddies were getting, asked, "How much didja pay for that oil, Dalton?"

"Twenty," said Dalton with a grin. "Wouldn't normally give a nickel for the oil, but that massage is gonna be worth it! Get in line, Wally."

Looking to his right, Wally whispered, "Here come the girls! An' they're just wearing shirts!"

Mike, turning to Ed, snickered, "This is gonna be epic."

"Look where they're gonna spread out!" Ed whispered back, already becoming excited with typical adolescent-male hormonal expectations.

As the girls were spreading their towels onto plastic lounges a few feet from the pool, Dalton whispered, "That's a perfect location. Once they lay out, Wally, you cannonball from this side and I'll get Two-Ton Logan to cannonball from the other side." Nodding, Logan, the two-hundred-and-thirty-pound center on the football team, and Wally moved into position for the coordinated stunt.

Still doing their best to ignore their male classmates, Cherie and the others were arching their backs and lifting the bottoms of their T-shirts to expose their bellies to the Florida sun.

All the while, from the concrete apron at the shallow end of the pool, Coach Buttito moved his tongue slightly across his lips as he watched the girls lie back. Despite the fact that he had sunglasses on, anyone observing him would have had no difficulty in determining that he was lusting after the hot teenage bodies.

At a prearranged signal, Dalton commanded "Go!" Wally and Logan made two long strides and leaped into the pool, creating two huge waves that drenched the unsuspecting girls and soaked their cotton t-shirts. With girlish shrieks, the girls' breasts were clearly visible under the saturated fabric. The splash, combined with the screams, caused immediate commotion. Nearly everyone in the proximity of the pool stared, the boys, of course, gawking the most.

Still screaming, the girls stood up and looked at each other, their breasts revealed by the cool water trapped in skin-tight cotton. As Angela looked at Cherie, her eyes got big, and then, looking down at herself, she crossed her hands over her prominent dark nipples, gasping, "Oh my God!"

Quickly aware that everyone at the pool was looking at them, Stacy pulled her shirt away from her body, rolled her shoulders inward, and grabbed the nearest towel. At the same time, Angela jumped into the pool, staying submerged up to her neck.

"Come here now, out of the pool!" an overweight mother yelled at two middle-school-aged boys. With goggles on their freckled faces, the two heads turned toward the girls, and their mouths dropped open.

Meanwhile, Kelly, who had been positioned far enough away so that she had not been affected by the splash, peeked over the top of her book, rolled her brown eyes, flipped her hair over her shoulder, shook her head at the commotion, and returned to her copy of *Lady Chatterley's Lover* again.

Stacy, safely covered with a towel, snapped, "I knew the perv posse was up to something!" as the boys snapped pictures with a couple digital cameras. In a flash, the entire contingent of horny males from Sherman Shifflett Memorial High School was getting the peep show they had been hoping and planning for.

Dalton exclaimed, "the pictures will go viral!" as Coach Buttito slid his glasses down his nose for a clearer view. Struggling out of his folding lounge, he approached the girls, his eyes frantically trying to see everything at once.

"Girls, cover yourselves!" the fat mother shouted once she had her two boys out of the pool, their faces pressed up against her large inner tube of a belly. While this was happening, Dr. Asbergski was still evidently snoring away in his room, and Athletic Director Butcher was sitting at a table in the coffee-and-breakfast bar at the other end of the resort. Her cell phone rang; she glanced at the caller ID number and mumbled out loud to herself, "It's the school," and then into the phone, "AD Butcher, how can I help you?"

The voice of the county superintendent demanded, "What is going on down there, Butcher!?"

"Huh? Whaddya mean?" asked the athletic director, completely alarmed by the unexpected mid-morning call.

"I just got a call from the mother of one of your female students that you have a durn wet t-shirt contest going on at the pool! Who the heck is in charge down there?!" shouted the superintendent.

Barely able to speak, Butcher replied with what she hoped sounded like respectful urgency in her voice, "Sir, I'm investigating and will report back in thirty minutes!" She hung up and mumbled to her girlfriend, one of the high-school gym teachers, "I shoulda known better than to leave Buttito in charge. That incompetent buffoon's glass is half empty and about to evaporate. Hurry, we've gotta get to the dang pool!"

Meanwhile, things were still very interesting at the poolside.

Chapter 12 Choices

November 22, 2015 - 0800 HRS

Benedict looked away from the monitor and shook his head.

"No. I would rather have one death on my conscience than what might be thousands!"

He put his hands over his face and Melik said, "FIRE!" Through his fingers, Benedict looked up to see blood spatter hit the window and his friend's body disappear from view. Benedict had made his choice. The guilt had just begun.

"Throw him back in the chamber! This time, set the temperature at twenty. Leave him naked and tied to the chair. Let him feel the ice form on his skin. Mist the chamber every fifteen minutes. Offer him the opportunity to change his mind every fourteen minutes," Melik snarled.

Zip-tied by his ankles, wrists, and neck to the metal chair, Benedict could not move. As the clouds of mist from the ceiling covered his naked body, his skin slowly turned purple and his eyes began to close under the film of the ice. Toes and fingers, white at first, began to turn blue; then, slowly, the freezing temperatures wiped away his body's warmth and moved to his core. Hypothermia overtook his body in minutes. To Benedict, it all seemed like a lifetime. Muttering to himself, he pleaded, *"God, take me. Let me die rather than be responsible for massive death."* After an hour of the torture, Benedict was unconscious, a thin film of ice covering his body.

The observing guard radioed to Melik, "He is unconscious, pulse rate is dropping, now at 49 bpm."

"Remove him from the chamber," Khayyam replied, "he will do us no good dead." "Place him in a warm bath," Melik commanded with urgency. "Inform me when he regains consciousness."

In a tub prepared with water at room temperature, Benedict's body temperature slowly began to rise. The warm bath stimulated his circulatory system and he began to shiver, blue lips returning to a pale red as his eyes opened and he became conscious, able to recognize his surroundings. He shook his head back and forth and rubbed the pain in his arms and legs, trying to get feeling back to his extremities.

Melik suddenly entered the room, the same one he had been in before being taken back to his cell. Melik commanded, pointing to the tall cart with the video monitor. "Turn on the live feed and let our guest watch."

On the large screen, Benedict saw the front of Partridge Hall, his daughter's college dorm at Bowdoin, where the quality of education was second to none. Many applied to the relatively small college; few were accepted. Sarah's gift was music. She could sing and play the piano, modern jazz her favorite genre. Benedict would listen to her for hours when she practiced at their home. She had a natural gift, even though no one else in Benedict's immediate family had talent like his Sarah. She was accomplished well beyond her adolescent years. Benedict loved his girl more than anything.

"Now, Dr. Arnold Benedict, do you recognize this school?"

Teeth chattering, he muttered, looking down, "Yes."

"Now let's see what you will choose next. Will it be your Sarah's life or a little assistance to my people? My soldiers have been watching her for days. We know her routine. So, Dr. Benedict -- life or death? We have placed a bomb on your daughter's Jeep Liberty fuel tank, that little SUV you bought her for her eighteenth birthday. The explosive is remotely activated. Her last class today ends in ten minutes. In about fifteen minutes, your daughter will start that little powder-blue Jeep. You can imagine what can happen next with a word from me. Again, your choice, Dr. Benedict."

Thoughts raced through the scientist's mind. *"God, please, not Sarah, I cannot allow these evil bastards to take my sweet little girl's life. What do I do? Sarah's life gone or thousands of people, individuals I do not even know, will die. Please, God, forgive me."*

He looked back up at the ruthless and heartless fiend. "All right, I will show you the procedure of how to reform a gene using a manufactured messenger RNA. Melik, I am begging you, do not lay a hand on Sarah!"

Melik smiled. "That's a much more cooperative attitude. I thought you might come around to see our urgency to kill our enemies. Your daughter's life will be spared; however, the bomb will remain on that little Jeep. This is just an insurance policy, you understand, in case you change your mind. However, since I am a family man, too, we will remove the explosive device after our enemies are destroyed. So, Doctor, do we now have your full cooperation?"

"For God's sake, yes! I will not design the virus; I will only share my procedure with you. What you do with my knowledge is your immoral decision. Not mine!"

"Immoral? Hardly. It is our *moral* duty to destroy those who seek to destroy us. Let us begin…with your cooperation…and with your daughter's safety in mind, lest we forget."

Chapter 13   Bloody Bus

April 20, 2018 - 1100 HRS

Angela and Kelly zipped up their travel bags and stormed out of the hotel room. Still fuming, Kelly, with *Carry-On* blush suitcase in hand, slammed the door and stomped down the carpeted hallway.

"That dang Dalton and the perv posse cut our senior trip short by a day just so they could see our breasts! If that was all they wanted, I would have just flashed them a personal peep show by pulling up my shirt!" she grumbled.

Angela pressed the elevator call button; instantly the door opened. Leaning on the elevator walls were Ed and Wally. Ed giggled and placed his fist over his mouth as his shoulders quivered. Wally turned red and looked straight down at the floor.

"What are *you* laughing at, you freakin' pervert?" Kelly fired, her eyes intense with anger. Ignoring Kelly, Ed made eye contact with Angela. "Durn girl, you have a nice pair. Just like tiny little melons!"

Angela nearly lit up with an appreciative smile, then caught herself, "Shut up, Ed," she muttered unconvincingly.

Finally reaching the first floor, the four exited into the nautical décor of the hotel lobby. The rest of the senior class was there, sitting on suitcases and backpacks, waiting for the tour bus that would take them home. Disappointed grumbling washed through the crowd as the few that had caused the early departure hid in the corner.

Coach Buttito, shouting unnecessarily loudly, called, "Get your bags an' load 'em under the bus bays where the driver's standing. Backpacks get placed in the overhead bins. No exceptions!"

AD Butcher, already agitated, in a deep tone, commanded, "Hurry up. Departure in five minutes!" Asbergski, picking up papers off the carpet and searching frantically for the bus manifest, yelled out, "Everybody, give me your disposable key cards, I need everyone's disposable keys." Students either didn't listen or just ignored him as they tossed their plastic key cards into the nearest trash cans.

Finally, all forty settled themselves into their seats, preparing for the twelve-hour bus ride back to Virginia. Once all passengers were situated in the vinyl seats, the bus driver accelerated up the on-ramp, following the blue sign for *I-95 North*. As the bus began to cruise the interstate, a few kids fell back to sleep, while others with headphones on had their eyes glued to Stephen Spielberg's 1985 *Goonies*. Giggles and chuckles echoed throughout the bus. "I love this part," was heard more than once. On the screen, the students watched Chunk pull his shirt up and began the legendary *Truffle Shuffle*. Hearing shouts of "Hey, you guys!" Mr. King, the driver, was pleased that the high school teens were enjoying his choice. For some kids, the movie provided some comic relief and took their thoughts away from getting their senior trip cut short.

In his seat, a distant blank stare on his face, Wally's hazel eyes had suddenly turned completely red. Noticing the startling change,

Ed whispered, "Wally, did Mentiroso give you something?" Getting no response from his friend, Ed turned to Mike, across the aisle, "Hey, Mike, I think Wally's trippin'."

Taking his eyes off the monitor above him, Mike looked at Wally. "Hey, Wally, what's wrong?" As the morning light shone through the bus windows, both Ed and Mike could see that Wally's face had broken out in sweat.

Without responding to either boy, Wally suddenly released a large volume of gas from his bowels, followed by bloody diarrhea that quickly filled his underwear and jeans. The pungent odor of bloody stool was nauseating as the students closest to Wally began grabbing their noses and covering their faces. Wally bellowed like an injured bear as others clawed at windows to open them. Their fear was almost tangible as it ripped through the bus. In the commotion, Wally's classmates heard a desperate cry for help. "Why is this happening to me? Why me?"

Charging to the back of the bus, Asbergski shouted, "Dalton, what is going on? What is going on?!" assuming that Dalton had something to do with this latest commotion.

"We don't know! Wally's got diarrhea again!" Dalton, confused and scared like the rest, shouted back.

One step behind Asbergski was AD Butcher, trying to evaluate what was happening to Wally, who lay on his side in the fetal position. Observing his bloodshot eyes, Butcher, a college athletic trainer before accepting the AD position, called out to no one in particular. "What drug did this kid take?" to which Dalton replied angrily, "Wally does *not* do drugs!"

Slowing the bus down safely, pulling onto the shoulder, and waiting until the air brakes had completely stopped the bus, King unbuckled his seat belt and raced back to the middle of the bus. Overhearing the AD's question, King observed, "Honey, I've seen all types of drug reactions in my day and this ain't from nothin' that can be bought on the street. I don't know of any kinda drugs that make someone doo doo…except for laxatives- an' they don't do this! This boy is very ill an' he needs immediate medical attention." With a spin and a few steps toward the front, King was on the radio and calling for an ambulance, giving the 911 dispatcher their location on the interstate. Listening intently to King, the dispatcher, asked "Do you think he needs a helicopter unit?"

At the same time, a state police officer had seen the bus, its hazard lights flashing, and had pulled over behind the bus. Pounding on the door, he entered and began scanning the seats as he listened to King. The officer's eyes stopped and focused on the students in the aisle by Wally's seat. Pushing the students away, he quickly observed Wally, who now had streams of dark red blood running from both sides of his mouth. Reaching with his left hand, he pulled his shoulder mike to his mouth and commanded, "We need a medical chopper now! Two miles south of exit 116. Tour bus on the shoulder. Adolescent male down, appears to have a severe abdominal bleeding. Very light pulse, but alive. Hurry, this boy needs immediate medical care!"

Suddenly, several female screams rose above the chattering voices as Buttito and three other boys on the bus started to trickle blood from their noses. Most of the males on the bus were in clear view of the state police officer who looked up from Wally and began scanning the passengers again. Just the four were bleeding, but the volume of blood coming from noses and mouths had suddenly increased. "Get something to cover their bleeding! Does anyone have ice?!"

Coach Buttito, in obvious pain, shouted, "My knees are tingling! It feels like little bubbles are popping in my knees!"

The other three boys were moaning and groaning.

"My elbows, my ankles! It's excruciating, like needles!" Another one screamed, "I can't move my arm!" as bystanders began to see the victims' joints expanding. "My head is killing me," moaned Buttito, the pressure in his brain had become too great, causing blood to begin gushing out of his ears as he took in a huge gasp for air. And then he was gone, a crumpled heap on the bus floor.

AD Butcher and the state police officer begin checking pulses but within seconds, Buttito and the three boys were dead, lying in pools of blood. The other students retreated to their seats in a panic, the faces of the victims completely white, drained of blood, eyes wide open, pained expressions remaining. The state policeman, fearing some kind of air-borne contagion from the blood, ordered everyone off the bus.

Within minutes, a helicopter arrived in the field next to the interstate. The paramedics entered the bus and removed the four bodies on stretchers, then attempted to evaluate the situation. After a few minutes of discussion and communication with hand-held radios, they ordered everyone back on the bus.

Confused and angered by the death of friends, Mike yelled, "Hell, no!" Dalton and all of Cherie's friends were shaking their heads. "No way. They're dead, and something on that bus must've killed them!"

The paramedic turned and spoke to the state police officer, who now had been joined by two other uniformed cops. "This is a potential quarantine situation! At the moment, we have no idea what we are dealing with! All people must get back on the bus now, please!" the paramedic announced. The policemen, arms extended, frantically began trying to herd the passengers back toward the open door of the bus, led by a tall, muscular state trooper. The other officers followed and repeated the order as they herded the kids back onto the bus.

Dalton, still shaking his head, yelled with a stubborn, "No!" and continued to back away. One of the officers pulled his taser from his belt and threatened to use it. Reluctantly, Dalton shuffled back to the bus, followed by a few other hesitant students.

Back on the bus, the paramedic, whose name plate read *Elijah,* radioed back to his hospital, "We need a HAZMAT team. We have several victims, deceased, showing similar symptoms. All very bad hemorrhaging from all observable orifices! The worst I've ever seen. It appears to be systemic and not isolated to one body biome. Requesting a precautionary quarantine and a team standing by for our arrival."

Meanwhile, the students and adults on the bus sat in stunned silence as they listened to Elijah's communication and stared at the pools of blood in the aisle of the bus, the putrid odor of evacuated bowels hanging in the air. The class trip that everyone had complained about ending with a lustful splash was now burdened with something much worse.

Chapter 14 Eyewitness Account

April 19, 2018 – 1810 HRS

Caleb Turner, the meteorologist for FOX 5 in Atlanta, began a segment on Hurricane Annie. His eyes intense under perfectly trimmed eyebrows, he announced, "Folks, we have a very strange weather pattern and not good news for this hurricane, and it's only the first Atlantic one of the season! Annie has followed the path of Katrina, not as big in diameter, but with a bigger punch of 127-mile-per-hour winds expected to hit the coast. Storm surge will not reach into New Orleans, fortunately, when it makes landfall during low tide, so we expect that flooding will be less devastating. However, it is still a powerful hurricane and the governor of Louisiana has announced a mandatory evacuation all along the Gulf Coast. Thousands are traveling north......"

A close-up shot centered on news anchor John Cole as he interrupted Turner in mid-sentence. "We break in with a special report just in: a crowd of protesters has arrived near Turner Field!" His deep green eyes looked into the camera lens, giving viewers the feeling that they were having a one-to-one conversation, as if they were getting the latest rumor from a co-worker. "We have a correspondent on the scene, Ben Hiter. Ben, what is happening on Pollard Boulevard?"

The screen changed to show Hiter holding the mike chest high. With a quick nod to his cameraman and a slight adjustment to his ear piece, Hiter reported, "A DEA agent and two Atlanta police officers have been shot down by a twenty-six-year-old black man with an assault rifle. The suspect is believed to be part of a cartel running heroin up and down the East Coast. The citizens near the stadium have turned this event into what they believe to be another racially motivated shooting!" The camera changed to show an angry mob shouting, "Black lives matter!" Sporadic shots from somewhere could be heard in the background while Hiter ducked his head and took cover behind the news van, the camera suddenly showing a strip of asphalt and grass.

After half a minute, the camera shifted back to the reporter. In a low tone, nearly whispering, Hiter continued. "I have been told that the suspect, identified as Melvin JaPrince Henderson, was driving a tractor trailer full of heroin that has been followed from Baltimore harbor. The same truck was observed and documented over ten times in the last two months, taking the same route. Both the FBI and the DEA believed it was part of a widespread drug trafficking operation they have been watching for the last three years. We were told that although suspicions had been confirmed, not until recently did law enforcement have enough evidence to prosecute. Earlier today, an observant county deputy saw the truck on the side of I-95 South where the driver was changing a flat tire. The 21-year-old deputy noticed the name of the trucking company that matched a pre-shift briefing. Following police protocol and to avoid alarming the suspect, the deputy drove past the truck and then immediately informed dispatch. The message was relayed up the chain of command, and in minutes, the DEA knew about the shipment.

Almost immediately, helicopters were in the air and a dozen unmarked cars raced from north and south to the truck's location on I-95. Surprised and surrounded, Henderson jumped into the cab and emerged with an AR-15 assault rifle. The officers ordered the suspect to drop the weapon and get face down. Instead, the suspect fired at least a dozen shots, striking the DEA agent and the deputy, upon which all officers fired in return and killed the suspect. This seemingly execution-style killing, or what is commonly referred to as "suicide by cop," was captured on cell phones. A video of the entire incident has already made its way to social media and has gone viral."

All traffic on I-95 was stopped south of the tractor trailer. After all precautions were taken to establish a safe zone for citizens, the top DEA agent of the scene ordered the truck to be opened while a diesel forklift maneuvered around to the rear of the truck. The first four pallets were pulled off the trailer as a terrible fish odor bellowed out of the hot trailer, the stench making one agent vomit. With the first pallets removed, agents quickly discovered another twelve loaded with large bricks of heroin wrapped in heavy green plastic.

Suddenly, with the camera returning to Ben Hiter, horrified viewers watched as he grabbed his nose as a large droplet of dark-red blood dropped onto his shirt. Suddenly, blood began oozing from his eyes. The bleeding became even more profuse from his nose and eyes as a terrified look swept across his face as he gasped, "My knees and elbows are aching! Oh, God, it's excruciating." As more blood ran, his face began to drain completely of all color. The cameraman, frozen, still kept his camera on the reporter, who began a horrible moaning. Even more blood continued rushing from his mouth and nose until Hiter dropped to the ground in a lifeless heap. An entire national television audience sat stunned, staring at their video screens...and having no idea what was happening there on an interstate highway in Georgia.

Chapter 15 Emergency Room
April 22, 2018 – 0900 HRS

"Why me mommie?"

"Honey. I don't know," his mother murmured as she caressed his moist forehead. She turned slightly to Doctor Morris and the nurse. "What is happening to my boy?"

"I expect it's a virus. Other southeastern hospitals have contacted state health agencies and reported very similar symptoms," the doctor, dressed in his spotless white lab coat, responded to the tearful mother.

The mother had bloodshot eyes and a tormented expression. The doctor, nurse, and mother were staring at the helpless little ten-year-old. As the mother pushed his black bangs from his dark, distant eyes, she whispered loudly enough for the others to hear.

"Yesterday, he was playing soccer with his friends. He played a full sixty minutes and then had a nosebleed that we could not stop. Doctor, it couldn't be stopped! We tried to stop the bleeding…" Her voice cracked. Staring in despair at the doctor, her face blotchy red and eyelids swollen, she continued. "Why my boy, doctor?" The nurse patted the mother on the shoulder as the little boy's electrocardiograph screen slowly went to a flat line. The mother became hysterical and the nurse tried to console her, but she continued weeping and uncontrollably shaking. Finally, the mother screamed, passed out, and fell to the floor.

As he stepped out of the small hospital room, Doctor Morris heard his name over the hospital intercom. A female voice announced, "Code red, doctor report to the emergency room!" Being the only attending physician in the hospital at the time, he raced down the main hallway, pushed the swinging metal doors to see seven boys, all bleeding profusely, in the arms of parents. Then he heard sirens of three ambulances pulling under the canopy to the emergency entrance.

All medical staff froze. Comments rose throughout the staff. "What is going on? Is there a major disaster?" Sunday mornings were always low in patient volume at the small community hospital. On the previous Sunday, the staff had to stabilize a motorcyclist's leg for a Monday-morning surgery; once in a while, they had to treat a gunshot wound from a hunting accident, but no one on staff had worked a trauma like this. They were totally unprepared for an epidemic.

The oldest and most experienced emergency nurse yelled, "Call for backup. Someone get on the computer and initiate the emergency preparedness plan! Contact the hospital communication-and-information center and tell them to make an *all call*. We need everybody available at the hospital. Inform 911 dispatch they must begin critical divert. We are at full capacity already; send to University Hospital."

The lead nurse added, "Skip registration and initiate emergency protocol! Take these boys to the exam rooms, now!" The nurses began protocol, checking vitals and interviewing parents on the run as well as any of the boys that were able to talk.

The triage nurses reported to Doctor Morris, all five with the same report following their initial patient exam and interviews of relatives. All the victims were males and each complained of joint pain, dizziness with severe headache, nosebleed, and approximately ten to twelve hours of profuse and unstoppable bleeding. Recalling reports from other hospitals, Morris knew that in less than twenty-four hours, each victim would become completely unresponsive. An experienced trauma physician, Morris always waited for vitals and screening assessments and confirmed diagnosis by personal examination; he then prescribed the proper treatment plan for each of his patients. But this time, he had nothing. He knew they all were going to die. The best he could do was sedate and try to reduce the pain.

Back in the waiting room, screams from relatives and moans from the suffering males made it impossible to hear the dialogue on the television monitor. As each pair of eyes glued to the waiting-room monitor, the crowd grew silent as the newscaster began to describe the epidemic.

The anchor announced, "I must warn viewers that the following images are very graphic and bloody. We strongly encourage you to use discretion when viewing. Again, what you are about to view are horrifying images of humans suffering. In Florida, the lead guitarist from Cody Purvis's Country Band was overcome by the virus last night in Jacksonville. The fans watched the big screen as the guitarist began bleeding and dropped to the stage. Although not confirmed, it is believed that NASCAR driver Lee Wigal caused a seven-car pileup due to the disease. His crew chief reports that he lost control in Turn Three as he succumbed to the virus. He had pulled into the pit on lap 51 because of a severe nosebleed. His manager inserted two cotton balls in his nose and Lee returned to the track during a caution. His team and family are waiting at Fulton County Hospital for the medical staff to announce a diagnosis." As the images on the monitor became more real, the anxiety and fear in this hospital's waiting room became something almost tangible. The experienced veteran nurses began directing other healthcare workers to console the crowd. Despite all efforts, nothing could put them at ease; by now, everyone knew this mystery virus was widespread and, at this point, unstoppable.

The camera returned to the news anchor. "The growing number of victims is rising exponentially. The CDC is reporting a new viral strain never seen before and warning the public to stay at home. Make no contact with other persons complaining of these symptoms."

In disbelief and fear, mothers began holding their boys tighter. Fathers had their boys pressed to their chests, their arms wrapped around them as if that would protect their children from this unseen virus. The boys looked at their parents with eyes that seemed to ask, "Why me? Am I going to die?"

Chapter 16 Strike Three

April 22, 2018 - 1400 HRS

"Strike three!" the umpire bellowed and twisted his upper body with fist clenched near his ear. The batter kicked some home-plate dirt as he stepped out of the box, tossing his bat aside in disgust as that half of the inning ended without drama.

"Uncle Tristan, that was a nice slider. Broke eight inches off the plate. Number three hitter couldn't even touch that one!" blonde, seven-year-old Blake exclaimed, looking for his uncle's approval.

Dr. Tristan Snyder looked and smiled at Blake's wide green eyes under his blue *Gwinnett Stripers* hat. "Yep, you're right, little guy. That was a nasty pitch. Your dad has taught you well. You'll be throwing that pitch yourself before you get out of Little League. Just keep working hard, but keep your—"

"--Grades up, I know!" Blake giggled. Then proudly, he announced without boasting, "I made honor roll last report card!"

"Good job, Blake," Snyder flashed a wide smile as he patted his nephew on his shoulder.

At that same moment, the ring tone of "Take Me Out to the Ball Game" chimed on his cell phone, the caller ID listing "unknown caller." He pressed the green icon and immediately growled.

"NO! I do not want to buy a timeshare and I surely don't want to refinance. Who is this!?" he snapped.

"Alex Azar, Secretary of the Department of Health and Human Services," a deep voice replied. "You're on speaker, Dr. Snyder. With me is your director, Dr. Redfield. We are facing a potential biological meltdown in the United States. Currently, we have an outbreak in the South in Florida and Georgia. We need you in the briefing room ASAP."

"Yes sir," Snyder replied, his tone suddenly restrained and serious. "I'm in Coolray Park in Lawrenceville and can be at the CDC in ninety minutes."

"You don't have time to drive! We've lost over eighty males in the last twenty-two hours, all with the exact same symptoms!" the health official said in a commanding and stern voice. "Time is of the essence. This is real as it gets. A government chopper will be landing inside the stadium in less than fifteen minutes!"

As Snyder returned his cell phone to a jacket pocket, his nephew suddenly pointed to the ball field, pointing. "Why are the umpires holding the players in the dugout, Uncle Tristan? And why are there policemen on the infield?"

"I have a kind of emergency, Blake," he tried to explain over the loud chatter from the fans near them. Then, frowning at what was happening on the ballfield, "Did someone get hurt? Radio stunt? What's goin' on? Why are they holdin' up the game?"

The stadium announcer's voice crackled through the loudspeakers, asking the fans to remain calm, that there was an emergency. The rumble of thousands of voices soon became mixed with the sound of helicopter blades in the distance, getting progressively louder.

Snyder grabbed Blake's hand, lifted the boy against his chest, and swiftly began making his way down the steps and toward the nearest exit. Identifying himself to a police officer who asked for the scientist's credentials, the two were hustled toward the field gate beside the home team's dugout and then escorted to second base. The cacophony of voices from the stands got even louder with the arrival of the royal blue helicopter, marked CDC, as it landed in center field. The blades slowed to a low hum. Blake put his hand on his baseball cap before it could be blown off from the downdraft of the blades. Lowering Blake to the green turf, Snyder trotted toward the helicopter, instructing Blake to keep his head low. A crew member ushered the boy and his uncle up the steps and into the back seats of the helicopter. The door was slid shut and secured, the rotation of the chopper's blades accelerated, and the aircraft lifted off as the boy sat next to his uncle in wide-eyed fascination. Once in the air, Snyder began making phone calls. "Dr. Siribsndu, Leoni, I need you immediately to report to the briefing room and wait for me!" he ordered, extreme urgency is his voice.

"I'm at the pool with the kids, Tristan! And I have a sitter coming tonight. It's our anniversary!" whined Leoni, one of Snyder's assistants.

"I'm sorry, Leoni, but we have a real emergency, and we think this is a bad one. We're all needed-- now. Call your sitter and your husband!" Snyder replied, trying to keep any panic from his voice.

"Okay," Dr. Siribandu said with a resigned sigh. "I should be there in about forty-five minutes." Snyder said nothing more as he speed-dialed another number, this time for Dr. Lowenstein.

"Cat, it's Tristan. We're needed at the CDC right now. Urgent and potential Level Four!" Lowenstein was a dedicated virologist,

Snyder's most passionate colleague, who wouldn't need to call for a sitter. She had no husband, no family--just work. She traveled a bit, but only to the areas of the world experiencing lethal epidemics. Everything she did was a quest to find knowledge about the viral world.

"Tristan, I'm already here in my office and reading a paper on a retrovirus causing denatured enzyme activity that kills T-cells during HIV infection."

"Looking forward to discussing that over coffee someday," Snyder replied somewhat sarcastically. "Get to the briefing room, Azar and Redfield are already waiting there. I should be there in ten minutes, according to the helicopter pilot."

Snyder shut off his cell phone and looked out the window just as the rooftop helicopter pad on the CDC came into view over a line of trees.

"Uncle Tristan, am I gonna get home tonight?" The voice of his nephew broke into Snyder's troubled thoughts.

Chapter 17 The Briefing Room
April 22, 2018 - 1500 HRS

Minutes after landing, Snyder burst through the door of the briefing room, "We've got a really wicked one!" he announced to startled colleagues who had been arguing about whose job it was to empty the previous day's coffee pot.

Dr. Leoni Siribandu stared at the six-foot, four-inch man. "What? *Wicked?* I thought wicked had to do with witches. English is so confusing. Fourteen years in Sri Lanka private schools and six years at Harvard," she added, shaking her head.

Dr. Lowenstien interjected, "It means we have a potential Level Four epidemic, Leoni!"

"Oh. OH!" Siribandu's eyebrows arched across her forehead as she took a sudden step backward, nearly knocking a coffee cup off the counter. Nervously, she quickly ran her fingers through her straight black hair.

"Oh, don't worry, Leoni, you'll be okay. Remember, we've been training for just this kind of emergency. Trust me, you'll do fine on your first viral rodeo! I picked you because you're the one of the best virologists in forensic epidemiology," Snyder said, his brown eyes reflecting a warm smile. "All right, everyone, in the laboratory in fifteen!"

That time later, the glass walls reflected the team as they sat at a table in the biological laboratory located in the basement of the CDC. The laboratory was designed for complete containment of lethal contagions. As an additional safeguard, the concrete structure was underground and enclosed by six-foot-thick walls and ceiling. Well lit with LED lights, the working tables were stainless steel. The white tile floors mirrored the blue-tinted lights, giving the lab a somewhat ethereal feeling.

"It sounds hemorrhagic," Snyder informed them in his first statement about the virus. "First report was four dead on a school tour bus, all males. The only slightly good news is one victim is in critical condition but has remained stable for thirteen hours."

Tristan looked at his team. "The epidemic is infecting victims exponentially. From what we can surmise at this point, we calculate that one infected victim can infect a hundred or more before death. We have to assume, until proven otherwise, that transmission can be airborne and water-borne and can continue until victims are buried or cremated. We are seeing a 99.99% mortality rate. Currently, the infectious agent has only killed males. The only victim to survive infection is one seventeen-year-old male on the tour bus. Preliminary reports indicate that this is a new infectious agent that CDC has been unable to recognize, let alone identify. We have to gather all information available and become instant experts."

Snyder continued. "As I said, my initial hypothesis is that the virus is hemorrhagic. Symptoms are similar to Ebola or Marburg: bleeding, diarrhea, and extreme joint pain. Onset to death, however, appears to be much shorter than those diseases. Medical reports indicate mortality in less than twenty-four hours. We must have comprehensive blood samples and tests from all victims, whether dead or alive. As a team, we will need to make contact with internists and doctors in all emergency rooms and gather samples from the dead. The media must be informed with accurate information to avoid public panic. The only thing spreading faster than this virus will be rumors, misinformation, and fear. We have to get our hands on everything we can find about the epidemic. Everyone on that bus has to be quarantined, interviewed, and examined."

As his colleagues sat stunned, he continued. "Our next step is to backtrack along Interstate 95 and search for cases. The highest density of victims has been located near the interstate. Our investigation of this outbreak has to be very much like the investigation of a crime, consisting of detective work, following every plausible hunch while carefully collecting evidence. In forensic epidemiology, our criminal is the bug. Find the bug...how it got into humans...how it's transmitted. But it's not just the bug we're dealing with-- it's the people. We leave this afternoon. We'll have a mobile lab. Double-check equipment and inventory. Materials we'll need for the investigation include: swabs, vials, syringes, sterilized packets of silicone gel for collecting cultures of specimens. Most important, we must have sealed bio-hazard suits. Each of you inspect your own suit to prevent contamination. Make sure your suit is not damaged. We must be able to breathe for two minutes using the self-powered, air-purifying respirators and make certain there is a complete seal on your hoods. Until we know more about this bug, we take all possible precautions and zero chances. In the event that this contagion is airborne-transmitted, make sure your SCBA system is fully functional and operating perfectly. I can't afford to lose any of you! Okay, that's it. Let's get started!"

Chapter 18 The Hunt

April 24, 2018 - 0800 HRS

Snyder began the informational meeting. "Let's discuss the results of the interviews of the kids. We're looking for animals that the students may have come in contact with. My first guess is some organism in the Southern Baptist Resurrection theme park. At least, that seems most likely. However, the group came down from Virginia, so something actually in their hometown could be the source at this point. We are literally searching for a needle in a haystack. Everyone interviewed had the same basic story: seven males were infected on the same day. The time should be the first clue. The boys on the bus and the older males dying in Florida must have something in common. Insect bites or matching localities must be our first inquiry. One possibility is a zoonosis bug that could have jumped from an organism to humans. Dr. Siribandu, you go first."

Siribandu looked briefly at her notes and then cleared her throat. "Well, I interviewed Ed. I have a suspicion that there is a clue to be found at the Jungle Ride. Ed said it was very hot that day. He said that they ate and then spent a lot of time in line. Experiencing the Jungle River Ride, all were wet because of the misting machine. Ed noticed a somewhat dark-skinned man adjusting or repairing the misting system while they were under the shaded waiting zone. Of course, the mist wasn't the only thing getting them wet; they all were splashed in the rapids and waterfalls. The park had also added a special effect of having jungle natives shooting streams of water at the thrill seekers to mimic indigenous warriors shooting blow darts. My wild imagination tells me that one or more of the supposed natives could be a terrorist, foreign or domestic, using some kind of biological agent in the water shot from the blowguns, but how the agent wouldn't also affect the shooter is beyond me."

"Oh, please, that is ridiculous, Siribandu!" snapped Lowenstein. "Have you been reading comic books recently? Talking about a SWAG!"

Dr. Snyder ignored the remark and asked Siribandu to continue.

Tactfully avoiding any response to her colleague's tactless remark, Siribandu continued. "Ed also stated they saw a rat eating some leftover food near the trash can. The food may have been rotting or somehow contaminated with something. Maybe it is a form of Hantaan, you may recall, similar to the one found by Ho Wang Lee in Korea. On that occasion, it caused the Korean hemorrhagic fever that infected American soldiers during the Korean War. We lost four hundred soldiers because of that rat virus," she added, looking around at the others at the table.

"Good observation, Leoni. We need to investigate that for similarities," said Snyder with a nod. Turning his head, Snyder asked, "Dr. Lowenstein, what did you find out from the girls?"

Like her Indian colleague, Lowenstein consulted her notes. "Well, according to the ladies, those boys – to use their words -- are a bunch of devious little doo doos. The girls told me about the free day at the swimming pool. As for the source of the virus, I don't have a theory. We know of nobody bitten by an insect or anyone who came in contact with avian or mammal species. Nothing suspicious at all. Other than hearing about the girls being upset about losing the last day of the senior trip, my interview provided nothing, just meaningless information about overly hormonal boys creating a wet T-shirt contest. The pool is negative for vectors," Lowenstein concluded.

Snyder snickered a little. "Oh boy, boys will be boys," he said with a wry grin. "All very interesting but no help to us. In support of your statement, a lack of a theory to any potential host continues to be a popular answer that gets us nowhere." Dr. Snyder leaned forward and placed his elbows on the table, running his fingers through his thinning hair. A few moments of uneasy silence passed until he looked up and continued.

"As for me, I interviewed Cherie, Wally's new girlfriend," Snyder added. "I felt that the closest person to the first victim was a good candidate to question. She shared an interesting observation about the Prospect Rock Restaurant. While in line, she said, the girls came in contact with a rat that ran right between the kids' feet as they waited in line. Also, there was heavy mosquito activity while they sat in the outside eating area. So, we need to capture several species of rodentia and the specimens Culicidae family, mosquitos."

Dr. Lowenstein interrupted. "I also interviewed Mike, the one the girls called "the biggest perv."

Siribandu and Snyder laughed, surprised at her use of the girls' slang. Lowenstein never talked about people, as indicated by her usual comment when the break room gossip starts: *Little minds talk about people, medium minds talk about events, and great minds talk about ideas.*" Never engaging in gossip, Lowenstein only talked about the cellular world of viruses. She continued, "It appears that the boys broke into the abandoned Hebron Theater where Mike came in contact with a bat that bit him. That implies the possibility of rabies or even Ebola!"

"My God, if this thing is Ebola, we're looking at a potential pandemic!" Snyder gasped, stunned.

Siribandu, her dark eyes wide with shock, swallowed hard and then took a deep breath. "God help us if this is airborne," she said in a hushed voice. "How was the contact made?"

Lowenstein continued. "Ed opened a trunk and a bat either flew out or dropped from somewhere above them. It got tangled in Mike's hair. Ed reported that Mike began running around the stage and screaming 'Get it out, it's going to bite me!' Ed found a stick, a cane or something from the theater set, and hit the bat while still on Mike's head. Blood dripped down Mike's face, but they weren't sure if it was his or the bat's."

"We have to capture the bat!!" Snyder said. "If it is of genus *Myotis*, the harmless brown bat, that should be no problem. At worst, Mike could have rabies. Hypothesizing, if it is the common brown bat carrying the virus, then we are facing a possible mutated Ebola. But if the bats in the abandoned facility are hammer-headed fruit bats, those flying rats must be an invasive species, maybe brought in on a fruit shipment from Africa. As you know, they get large numbers of shipments from the African continent down here. Friends, if we capture *Hypsignathus monstrosus,* we have a strain of Ebola. This finding would be conclusive, in that Ebola hides in the order Chiroptera. Virologists have had this hypothesis for thirty years. If we find positive evidence for Ebola, that supports the theory that the transmission hosts are bats. We need to move fast. Load the mist nets and the fifteen-inch Sherman box traps. We need all creatures alive to bring back to the lab for fresh tissue to be tested. We need to leave right away for the amusement park. Be on the roof for helicopter departure in thirty minutes," Snyder directed as the others quickly picked up their notebooks and coffee cups and hurried out of the room.

Chapter 19   O-Type Blood Group
April 23, 2018 - 0800 HRS

Meeting in the glass office downstairs in the CDC, the team gathered to formulate a strategy to stop the virus and hopefully halt the growing panic and fear across the country. This time, more scientists had joined the briefing. Several federal and military officers were in attendance as well, listening to the scientists' conversation, while other officials were viewing the meeting via video from Pentagon headquarters.

Snyder, dressed in his jeans and tugging on his sport-coat collar, cleared his throat and began. "The evidence is clear that the pathogen is not bacterial or fungal. We have ruled out Ebola and Hanta. This mystery microbe does not follow anything we have observed in previous pathogenic studies. It definitely is hemorrhagic; full systemic onset produces more profuse bleeding than Ebola. At this point, we must accept that it is a virus, a cruel airborne virus selecting its host, most specifically males. Dr. Lowenstein, do you have anything to add?" he asked, turning to the brilliant female scientist as Dr. Azar made eye contact with her.

"The collection of data indicates that the virus infects primarily males of all age groups," Lowenstein stated as she stood. "Death is fast. In every case, it occurs in less than twenty-four hours. It would seem, however, that viral infection might occur faster from initial exposure. Mortality rate remains 100%. The only exception is the one boy on that tour bus in Georgia."

Dr. Siribandu interrupted, "And without exception, the autopsies indicate that all males had O-type blood."

Azar respectfully questioned Snyder, eyes wide and troubled to hear the information. "Are we sure about this?"

"Yes, every medical report has shown O-type blood, every victim," Snyder affirmed.

"We must classify this virus," Alex Azar demanded.

"I already have," Dr. Siribandu specified.

"She has spent every minute since returning from Orlando trying to identify this bug," Lowenstein announced. "Pull your image onto the screen, Leoni."

Dr. Siribandu moved her fingers swiftly across her keyboard. In two seconds, she opened her image file and selected her scanning electron microscopic specimen. The virus appeared on the screen, a three-dimensional image on both the briefing and Pentagon screens. "This pathogen is clearly a membranous enveloped virus. You know, the same structure as HIV."

"A retrovirus!?" the national health secretary remarked, a startled look on his face.

"Yes, it has the circular shape, protein-covered capsid," Dr. Siribandu assured the Secretary of the Department of Health and Human Services and the accompanying military leaders. "We have named the virus, YMe! because, as you are now aware, it only infects males!

Azar turned to General Johnson. "My God! It's airborne *and* a retrovirus," he gasped, totally shocked by the news.

General Johnson looked at Alex Azar. "What does this all mean? Somebody drop the science terminology and tell me what we are facing!"

Dr. Leoni added, "Medical reports state that human symptoms are similar to hemophilia."

"What!?" Azar asked, shocked even more by the additional findings.

Looking at the top brass on the Pentagon screen, Dr. Lowenstein began to explain. "HIV makes contact with T-lymphocytes. The HIV virus only infects T-lymphocytes. Our preliminary studies believe this monster, the YMe virus, is targeting platelet cells and inhibiting clotting in only males! At the moment, we have no way of stopping this evil biological creature and believe it is a manufactured virus created through genetic manipulation."

Looking directly at the large screen, Siribandu asserted, "This is certain to be a pandemic. Forty percent of the world's population has O-type blood. This will kill a thousand times more people than the influenza of the twentieth century. It has already hit Orlando International Airport and the summer vacationers at the Southern Baptist Resurrection theme park, where we believe it was somehow released. The park location alone has exposed twenty thousand possible hosts. And without being insulting, we are wasting time talking to you. We must get back into the lab!"

Without hesitation, Snyder jumped from his leather office chair and sprinted out of the meeting room. General Johnson, viewing the large screen, bellowed, "Where the heck is he going?"

Dr. Azar, confused, shouted, "Dr. Lowenstein, we need him! This is developing into a biological meltdown. Where is he going?" Azar stared, eyes wide open, surprised by Snyder's impulsive behavior in the moment of crisis.

Siribandu looked at Lowenstein with a shoulder shrug while Lowenstein glanced back at the screen one last time and stated, "We will contact you in thirty minutes."

"Wait, wait, this is not a …." someone in the Pentagon audience began as the screen went to rainbow-colored bars.

"Where did he go?" someone in the meeting room asked.

Dr. Siribandu responded, pointing in the direction of the elevator, "Tristan went to the elevator!"

Chapter 20 Oval Office
April 24, 2018 - 1100 HRS

General Johnson rushed past the Marine guard and burst into the Oval Office.

"Mr. President, we are under attack!" he shouted, interrupting the President as he was on the phone congratulating the coach of the West Virginia Mountaineers basketball team for their first NCAA title.

The President dropped his pen on his desk and, quickly recovering his composure, demanded, with tightened jaw muscles, "Where? What country?!" Before Johnson could reply, the President spoke into the phone, "I'm sorry, Coach, something urgent has come up! I'll have to call you back!"

General Johnson, with the health department secretary rushing in behind him, said, "We need to brief the Cabinet and the Joint Chiefs. It's an epidemic! The C.I.A. has determined that that maniac Quibt is behind the outbreak and death!"

The President, his eyes wide, shouted, "How is that possible? Did that bastard cause the epidemic in the southeast?!"

"The scientists said that the virus was manufactured, and that the evil sonofabitch has programmed a virus to infect American males. The infectious agent is targeted toward our boys, possibly killing all ages, infants to ninety plus!" the general replied, the vein on his forehead pulsating. "Jesus, thousands have already died and it appears thousands more will follow!"

The President blinked his eyes as his left eyebrow lifted into an arch. "What do you mean? What are you saying? Our intel said his group has only a hundred men at most who could spread the disease. How could intelligence command miss this!?"

"No excuses, sir, our intel showed no indication of a biological attack on the American public. We were completely blindsided. After a thorough investigation on all accumulated chatter in the last four years, nothing indicated grounds for suspicion. The terrorist cell was nonexistent until Quibt's contact with the embassy in northern Iraq, a region heavily populated by the Kurds. The message from Quibt was given to the Kurd ambassador, who contacted our ambassador. He is on his way now to the White House."

"Can we get more details from the Kurd ambassador?" asked the President.

"No, not possible. He was shot in the head shortly after he made contact with us. The bastards murdered his entire family in their home while sleeping!" the general responded angrily.

"How do we stop further spread of the virus? We must stop it now!" the President shouted some more, slamming both fists on the desk that Lincoln and JFK had both sat behind.

"The CDC has their best team working on this, sir," Johnson replied.

"Hell, they better have everybody in Atlanta focused on the epidemic. We have to find a way to stop this. What is Fort Derrick doing? They spend millions on research and experimenting with monkeys. Are they finding anything or do they have any idea how to stop this biological attack?"

Johnson shook his head. "Sir, I am deeply saddened to report that our best virologists have not found a way to stop the epidemic and our best physicians do not have a treatment available for the infected males. In other words, any infected boy or man will die in twenty-four hours, bleeding profusely in the last half hour. At this rate, the epidemic will be a pandemic within days. All countries are facing massive mortality. Never has death on this scale been seen before, not even with the black plague in the Middle Ages. Quibt has the free world in a death grip!"

Letting out a long, wavering breath, the leader of the free world looked around the room and asked, "How can I talk to Quibt?"

No one answered.

Chapter 21 Bow to Allah

April 25, 2018 - 1000 HRS

"The Earth will bow to Allah. The Divine Prophet has given me the power to bring North America, all of Europe, Asia, South America, and Australia --- all the world and all humans -- to be under the power of the supreme deity, Allah. The only God! World-worthy Lord! The true Alpha Omega! My omnipotent Lord has given me the authority to be the King of the World. My army will not stop until there exists total Islamic world domination!" Spit sprayed from his thin, serpentine lips. "I will continue to build a mighty army by making your armies surrender to mine! My military will dictate every law. The feeble nations of Africa and the Middle East will follow. These people were the believers of Allah since the beginning. These nations are promised rewards for service to Allah. Our brothers of Muhammad will be rewarded for honoring the divine message in the *Quran*, the only recognized holy book! This is my proclamation! The world will obey!" he shrieked.

The President and the Joint Chiefs of Staff sat looking at the giant screen as the hairy, swarthy Quibt glared into the screen with evil dark eyes, standing in front of a wall of orange flames.

"The world population cannot fight against the power of Allah. Cairo is the new caliphate. As servants of Allah, the ultimate power will control all economies. All the world is under the command of Islam. The holy religion! The Western influence and its control of the Suez has never been forgiven and will cease existing from this moment forward! Your Western ideas have polluted the Islamic way of life, but no more. The heathen West's way of life will be forever forgotten! Democracy and capitalism shall be erased from history! My divine power has been demonstrated. Allah has given me the power of Moses. The power of the Caliphate has released the plague. My followers, armed with my mighty power, have killed millions of males with O-type blood. Immediate submission and surrender is your only option. As you have seen in recent days, my scientists have the knowledge to design viruses to kill anyone, at any time. Any refusal to obey, any rebellion, will be crushed with extreme prejudice and without mercy. The DNA from each nation of people has common traits and these homologous characteristics will be used to exterminate all who refuse to surrender to Allah.

Any protests will be stopped with terrible death in massive numbers. Everyone on Earth will honor and serve Allah. Begin now! Every knee will bow to Allah. Followers of other religions will face death. Nations that refuse to follow these conditions will see their citizens continue to die. Surrender to the Caliphate. Refuse and you will find that destruction and death will follow, and soon!"

The madman paused for a moment to gather his breath and then continued. "Every door on every building must show the symbol of Muhammad bowing to Allah… and on the entrance to every habitable space, every religious and educational institution, government offices, industrial facilities, and residences. The surrender symbol has been posted on Google at this moment; print it and place it on your door and your surrender will be recognized; you will be safe and my armies will not enter. Without this symbol, this acknowledgement of Muhammad, I have commanded my army to murder and burn. No hostages will be taken and the oldest individual of every family will be shot and nailed to the door of every infidel's house. There will be no exceptions.

"In addition, I demand the immediate surrender of all staff of the CDC in America. My scientists are in complete control of the deadliest virus known to man. Those resources will be used to exterminate any rebellion!" he screamed as spit again launched from his lips.

Quibt ended the communication without naming a deadline to his demands; all the screen showed was the scene of the burning children at the elementary school in Colorado weeks before.

In shock and rage, the President stood and shouted, "That evil bastard has declared victory in some kind of holy war! How are we going to stop this dictating maniac?!" Those in the room with him could do nothing but stare blankly at one another. No one spoke.

Chapter 22   DNA Collection

April 27, 2018 - 0900 HRS

Benedict was wrapping up the day and scrubbing down in the shower. Turning the water off, he overheard two scientists talking on the other side of the shower curtain, their voices echoing in the otherwise empty shower room. After recognizing that a few muddled words were in Arabic, he began to listen more intently.

"The Jama'at allkhwan al-Muslimin is claiming victory," he heard one say in heavily accented English, "the Caliphate has been established. Allah will have victory over the idolaters. The Western world will be ours in days. The Americans will fall. The blaspheming bastards have faced the power of Allah. All American males with O-type blood will be dead in days, their blood shed in the name of Allah!"

Confused and shaken, Benedict wondered, *"What has happened in America? Has there been a threat against the U.S. government or an attempt to overthrow the United States?"* Then he heard the lead

Middle Eastern scientist say, "In days, we will have the O-type blood virus ready to release. The United States will be history and the caliphate will be in full power and rule. Just like in the days of Moses, Americans will beg for their boys' lives while American women will be our slaves and bow to Islam!"

Horrified, Benedict realized that his process of retrovirus engineering had been used to create a virus with the mission to seek out and destroy American males, and his knowledge would be used to destroy the American life and its very existence.

"What do I do? How bad could this become? Forty-five percent of the population has O-type blood; that's approximately fifty-percent male! The country could potentially lose eighty million males. Oh God, what have I done by allowing these terrorist bastards access to my retroviral engineering? Dear Heavenly Father, please guide me. I came here to help a village and now my knowledge has been used by our worst enemy!"

Leaning against the wet tiled wall, his head pressed against his forearms and eyes tightly closed, Benedict meditated on Psalm 109, asking God to protect him from his enemies.

"I have to save America and potentially the Western world from these terrorists," he thought as visions of a worldwide holocaust flashed through his mind. Suddenly, a plan emerged.

"I know how to alter any virus and I've observed a phenotype common to all guards in the compound. There must be a homogenous phenotype or gene that is common. But what? If I can determine the common trait, I can wipe these bastards out from within. How can I get the common code? How do I collect the DNA needed to sequence it?" he thought as his mind raced.

In the most recent days, since the brotherhood celebrated their apparent victory, there had been limited moments that Benedict was not closely watched. He used his observational skills to look for predictable behavior patterns, determining that there must be inconspicuous means to collect different fluids and take the specimens back to the lab for analysis.

Back in his cell, he watched as Imran delivered all his meals. The tormenter would eat half of Benedict's food and then slide the rest under the bars of the small cell. He would laugh and only say, "Here is some of your meal," and then slink away with a sneer on his pock-marked face. Anticipating the routine, Benedict realized that the guard could supply his first and easiest specimen. His saliva would be on the straws and the spoons; a quick swab would provide a very operative sample of DNA to be placed into a specimen container when he had been led back to the lab.

Bilal, the second guard, was Benedict's usual escort to the shower in the mornings. Benedict had noticed that he kept a Victoria's Secrets catalog in one of the stalls and guessed that Bilal was not shopping for a wife but had simply found a way to have sex by myself while the scientist showered. The next day, Benedict waited in the shower until Bilal had left his favorite stall and locked the shower room door behind him as usual. Quickly, Benedict thumbed through the catalog and ripped a page spotted with Bilal's most recent ejaculation. A semen sample would provide a fresh and workable sample of DNA. Folding the soiled page, Benedict slipped it under the towel around his waist and then banged on the door, his signal to his guard that he was ready to return to his cell to dress.

Minutes later at the lab, he was able to collect the semen sample, put it in the specimen container, and seal it. He stored it in an inconspicuous space behind some boxes where no one would have reason to look, knowing that the terrorist virologists had to believe that he was still working on their biohazard sample. He remained in the lab until early evening, acting busy each time someone looked in to check on him and giving no indication that he had overheard the terrorists' plan.

Early the next morning, just as dawn was breaking, Quibt suddenly threw open the door to Benedict's cell. Smiling evilly, he sneered, "Soon all the O-type blood males will be exterminated in the United States. Your American males will be wiped off the planet forever. Your nation will soon be on its knees praying to the supreme Allah. We have tricked you and now your knowledge is at work to destroy America. You have made the Jama'at allkhwan al-Muslimin the most destructive biological agent in history. The American government already believes you are a traitor!"

Quibt's declaration ignited rage in Benedict, and he threw a punch directly into Quibt's face. Quibt's head was thrown back. Swiftly, the subordinate terrorists swarmed Benedict, knocking him against the concrete wall. Quibt commanded, "Let the American go!" The quick release gave Benedict one more opportunity to strike, but this time, expecting it, Quibt grabbed Benedict's flying right fist out of the air. Squeezing the fist, the terrorist leader scornfully snapped, "You fight like a girl!" Benedict's left hand, still free, raked across Quibt's face like a claw, leaving three wounds that quickly filled with blood. Quibt's followers howled in shock. Holding his hand to the wound, Quibt continued to sneer." The American fights like a kitty cat!" Failing to realize Benedict's intent, Quibt was ignorant of the fact that the American had been successful -- he now had a sample of Quibt's DNA under his fingernails, certainly enough for analysis. The terrorist laughed, but Benedict knew who had been the victor.

Chapter 23   Search for Ground Zero

April 28, 2018 - 1600 HRS

"This virus is unlike anything I have ever seen!" Dr. Lowenstein exclaimed in frustration, rubbing her eyes with both hands. "I've been analyzing the messenger RNA for hours and it doesn't match any nucleic strand or family of retroviruses known. It appears it just mutated out of nowhere! The gene locus is on the maternal X chromosome. The smaller male Y chromosome does not have an opposing gene. The male genome is completely exposed for viral attachment. Classic Darwin, the males are being selected out of the population!"

"It's the YMe virus! Could it be designed?" mused Snyder.

Dr. Siribandu pointed at her monitor with her index finger slightly curved, her eyes wide, and her attention totally focused on the screen. "We must analyze the data! We know that the virus attacks platelets and only in males with O-type blood. Hemorrhagic symptoms, bleeding is fast and furious." Leoni's jaw tightened. Almost tearing up, she added, "These boys are dying in less than twenty-four hours. We have to find a cure…or at least something that will give them a chance."

Her expression filled with compassion and the frustration of the others, Lowenstein nodded her head. "We must keep the emotions out of the problem. You're right -- the answer is in the data, which we have trained our entire adult life to trust. Start with what we *do* know: the platelets are responsible for regulating clotting of blood. Blood is a mixture of compounds, so it is either a liquid racing through the circulatory system, delivering and removing compounds necessary for life…or plasma that briefly turns into a solid to prevent bleeding. The infected males' blood liquefies; the viscosity is drastically lowered. Blood in a normal, functioning circulatory system is seventy-percent water. The males with the virus experience their blood averaging ninety-six percent water. The entire metabolic clotting system is disrupted. How could this happen?"

Snyder, with his head slightly tilted, repeated to the two other epidemiologists, "True, the metabolic clotting pathway is disrupted. That is an understatement, for in the late lysogenic cycle, it is completely inoperative. This engineered microbe is pure evil. This YMe virus kills and brings absolute fear to anyone observing an attack. The attack psychologically murders the witness, while it liquefies the infected victim. It's terror, pure and simple. Fear is the only thing spreading faster than the virus!"

Siribandu hesitated, then responded, "Dr. Snyder, you are personifying the viral agent. It is a viroid that uses platelet cells to reproduce. We must stick to the biology! The virus is composed of non-living organic chemicals and it certainly is not a thinking entity. The particle is made of only nucleic acid and protein, randomly bouncing around until it meets the receptor protein on the surface of the platelet cell membrane. It then attaches to the cell and injects its messenger RNA code, which corrupts the platelet genome. The metabolic signaling system is interrupted and the enzymatic clotting cascade completely denatured. In science, this is 'the black box.' It is our job to open it!"

"Okay, you're right," Lowenstein conceded. "Let's start from the beginning. Patient Zero must have the answer. The origin of the YMe virus is our key. We have ruled out the obvious zoonosis: rats, bats, and insects. Our tests show no natural vector. We know that the viral agent is airborne, but this is like searching for a grain of sand on Miami Beach!"

"True," agreed Snyder, "but when we try to track down the YMe virus itself, to be accurate, we may find the information we need. And, as we all know, all great epidemiologists find the viral origin, ground zero, by patient interviews. The people tell the story, they alone hold the key. The victims will give us strong clues. So let's talk and review the data we've collected." Slapping his hands on the table, he continued, "We've spent all our time focused on the amusement park and the Prospect Rock Restaurant. What else do the initial victims share in common? Think: what do people do during the day at an amusement park? We have to trace every step a park visitor would take during a visit. What else happened during their day? What else did the boys and the adult males have or do in common? All went to the park and later, to the restaurant. All victims succumbed to the virus on the same afternoon. All males had to come in contact with the virus at one location. Initial contact will be our best clue. The chronological intersect between them all is our biggest indicator! Pull the file notes on the adult males' families who were interviewed. First of all, where did the families stay?"

"Let me check," Dr. Lowenstein muttered, selecting the tab labeled "ADULT MALE, CASE NUMBER 8." Looking up in surprise, she exclaimed, "Tristan, the families all stayed at the same hotel!"

"Wait! Did all victims go on the Jungle Ride?" Dr Siribandu questioned.

"Yes," Lowenstein confirmed. "The report indicates that the group of kids with Wally and the adult male's families rode that particular ride on the same afternoon."

"Interesting," remarked Dr. Snyder, "but if you recall, the misting system came up negative. No evidence of viral dispersal. The pump system was clear. What else is in that construct that could harbor a virus?"

Dr. Siribandu started flipping through the files. "There's a record that all the victims but one were hit with the native blow darts!"

"Really?! Now I feel like I've been reading comic books again! I've heard it all. Darts?!"

Ignoring Lowenstein's remarks, Snyder said, "Dr. Siribandu, I'd like you to go back to the park and interview the jungle ride personnel. You seem to feel strongly about this, so follow your instincts! Besides, you might turn up something else while you're investigating. Meanwhile, Lowenstein and I will return to the hotel to go through the entire facility. What else does the report say? Is there anything else that could be common to all initial victims?"

Siribandu continued scanning the reports. "Well, this is interesting. It appears that an adult male's wife and Cherie both bought sunblock from the hotel gift shop."

"Hmm, very interesting," Snyder murmured. "I recall speaking with Cherie about that, too. Was that the sunblock that came with the erogenous rubdown or massage-- whatever they called it? Sounded to me like a pretty good deal…and cheap!"

"You're more perverted than the kids!" Lowenstein remarked.

Tristan raised and dropped his eyebrows three times with a little gleam in his eyes in the manner made famous by Tom Selleck on that detective television show.

"Well, the adult male's wife described the sunblock massage much differently, and I'm not sure if she was jealous or just plain pissed. I recall that she grabbed her two little redheads and went back to their room," Tristan added with a chuckle, Cat giggling a little when their eyes met.

Back to the seriousness of the matter, Tristan commanded, "Get your field equipment. We're joining Siribandu and all going back down to Florida!"

Comment []: originally was Kate? who is Kate?

Chapter 24 Death in the Compound

April 28, 2018 - 2200 HRS

A small SEAL team of six heavily armed reconnaissance specialists met Benedict at the front door of the old weather station. After Benedict identified himself and the circumstances that found him there, the team leader, with the rank of commander and his name, Blanchard, over his right chest pocket, moved in. Dressed in full combat gear, with eyebrows lifted and mouth wide open, he asked, "How did you get out? Our intel informed us that there were at least twenty unidentified intruders here."

Before the scientist could answer, a young man, rank E-4, who couldn't have been more than twenty-one or twenty-two and was dressed in combat fatigues with his 9mm Heckler & Koch slung over his right shoulder, jogged up and reported to another officer standing next to Blanchard. "Warrant Officer Kerns, body count is fourteen. Sir, all the dead including Melik are coiled in the fetal position and lying in pools of blood."

Blanchard did a head turn back at Benedict. "How the heck did that happen?"

"I engineered a virus that took out the compound," Benedict explained. "When the group took off their burnooses, I noticed they all had unibrows. This is a sign of a phenotype, a DNA strand of a specific gene. It was easy to isolate the sequence, and once I did, I was able to design a virus to infect them from inside the compound."

Without acknowledging an understanding, Kerns turned to the communications soldier and snapped, "Whatever. Call for transport now!"

Following orders, the young enlisted SEAL turned to the microphone on his right shoulder. "Target acquired and safe. Need transport for pick up, pronto!"

"How did you find me? And where am I?" Benedict demanded.

"Satellite surveillance after some local fishermen reported activity here, where no one was supposed to be. We tracked flights from the Middle East to here, and evidence of humans from markers using body-heat sensors. We were dispatched to find out who they were, because even though NORAD no longer uses this station, it is still off limits to any civilians.

Half an hour later, Benedict, safe in a Humvee, looked back and was startled by a white flash. The terrorist compound on a remote edge of Hudson Bay, housed in an abandoned weather station that had held him captive for so long, had been taken out by the Canadian Air Force in seconds.

Thirty minutes later, the team and the rescued scientist watched as a U.S. Air Force C-130 that had been standing by slowly coasted down to the remote runway. The rear hatch was lowered as three Americans in civilian suits made their way down the ramp. Without identifying themselves, they hustled Benedict aboard the transport plane. He barely had time to buckle into one of the seats along the inner fuselage before the plane turned, powered up, and took off, all within minutes of arrival at the remote airstrip.

On the long flight home, thoughts and questions raced through Benedict's mind. As he ran his fingers through gray, thinning hair, the comprehension that his knowledge had been used by fanatics to threaten the Western world had left an emptiness in his heart. The guilt of possible human death on a massive scale was becoming too much. *"How can I face my colleagues again, knowing that I was responsible for allowing such genetic power to fall into the hands of fanatical bastards? Will the American public find out and think I'm a traitor?"* he thought, the plane's four engines throbbing as it roared over the blackness of the Canadian landscape below.

Benedict woke from a troubled sleep as the aircraft touched down at Langley with the dawn sun casting long shadows over the field. Looking out the window, he saw vans from every major network, their satellite dishes on the roofs, all pointing up at the same angle.

"How can I avoid the questions? What do I say?!" Thoughts raced through his mind.

The head State Department officer sat down next to him, gripping his forearm firmly.

"We're hustling you off the plane and into a chopper. There's gonna be a lot of questions shouted at you. Don't say a thing. Our sole objective is to get you on that helicopter. Ready?!"

As they practically raced down the metal steps, Benedict saw flashes coming from every angle and a muddle of voices being drowned out by the slowly decelerating jet engines. Shading his eyes with his right hand as four soldiers escorted him and the other two government men to what he guessed was a Black Hawk, he saw that the blades were already turning slowly. A young crew member almost threw Benedict into a canvas seat and buckled him in as the rotors above them increased in velocity; then, they were off the ground, the pilot announcing, "ETA Pentagon, 1530 hours."

He was home...and somehow, alive.

Chapter 25 Lethal Lotion

April 29, 2018 - 1500 HRS

Stepping out through the sliding door of the mobile biohazard van, marked with the CDC emblem, both epidemiologists exited, carrying HAZMAT-collecting equipment in backpacks. Taking a deep breath and looking briefly at the deep-blue Florida sky, Snyder looked at Lowenstein.

"Let's go through the equipment checklist one more time: swabs, vials, syringes, sterilized packets of silicone gel, liquid nitrogen container," to which Lowenstein replied "check" each time. "If we find this virulent agent, it must be dry-shipped. We want the bug preserved and ready to transport to Atlanta. The last thing we want is an equipment mishap," Snyder finished, receiving an acknowledging nod from his partner. After inspecting their field equipment, they walked into the hotel lobby. Snyder told Lowenstein, "Go to the front desk and find the hotel manager; he should be expecting us. In the meantime, I'm going to the pool area."

"Got it. See you in a few minutes, Tristan," Lowenstein replied.

Snyder began walking toward the landscaped pool area, a simulated lagoon modeled after Jamaica's Montego Bay, not that he knew that. The addition of white sand and the crystal blue water made the swimming area a replica of a tropical paradise. Water slides were carved out of the artificial jungle forest, offering a cool splash into the still blue water. Snyder thought to himself, *"There's got to be a million possible places for this tiny monster to hide. Where are you, you little demon? I know you're in here somewhere!"* Just then, Snyder heard someone coming up behind him, interrupting his thoughts. Lowenstein called out, "Here we are. The manager and the head of maintenance are here, too." Turning around, Snyder responded, "Okay, okay. Do you have the list of questions?"

"Yeah, I'll pull them up on my iPhone." Lowenstein placed her index fingerprint on the homescreen button and the list of questions appeared. "First question -- and maybe maintenance can help with this one -- Have you had any complaints about insect infestation or pollution of any kind?" she asked the heavy-set supervisor.

The hotel manager interrupted, and turning to the chief maintenance employee, asked, "I'm not aware of any, are you?"

Wiping a sheen of sweat from his forehead, the maintenance chief shook his head as Lowenstein continued.

"Second question: do you recall seeing any people lingering around the pool during the day on April 17? You know, not swimming, but acting out of the ordinary?"

Again, the manager responded that there had been no complaints and no reports about suspicious characters who didn't appear to be guests. "I'll have to check with security, and we can certainly pull some video from that day. We have complete coverage of the pool facility…well, everywhere but the changing rooms, of course."

"Next request: can we get a bottle of the hotel sunblock? Several of the victims bought your sunscreen," Lowenstein continued.

The manager pressed his eyebrows. "What sunblock? We sell a *Hawaiian Tropic* lotion at the front desk, but nothing with the hotel logo on it."

"We heard from several guests that your establishment sold sunscreen and it came with a complimentary massage…uh…application by two, well, very pretty young women," Snyder informed the manager.

"What!?" The manager's whole body became tense. "We can investigate that, but I've been the manager for two and half years. We don't sell our own tanning products of any kind and especially do *not* offer messages around the pool…or anywhere else!"

Lowenstein persisted. "In all interview recordings, it was reported that the tanning oil in question was purchased at the Tiki hut. More specifically, there were two ergonomic massage tables and two well-tanned female employees in yellow bikinis that applied the tanning oil."

"Absolutely not! Those girls, whoever they were, don't work for us!"

Snyder, somewhat shocked, looked at Lowenstein. "Get Siribandu over here!" Then, turning back to the manager, said, "We must review what, if anything, those cameras recorded."

"Yes, sir, absolutely. Follow me," the manager replied. Raising his hand-held radio, he spoke quickly. 'Jones, pull up DVD of the pool area on April 17. We need to review all activity between 0400 to 2400 hours! We'll be right there, and I want video on all monitors!" The technician's reply crackled in the manager's ear.

Entering the back door of the hotel, the manager flashed his magnetic badge and flung open the maintenance department's metal door. He, Snyder, and Lowenstein, now joined by Siribandu, rushed down the steps. Again flashing his magnetic key to open another identical gray metal door, all four entered a stuffy ten-by-eight security room that housed several computer stations half-dozen tall, gray metal cabinets, and just as many file cabinets. Shoulder to shoulder, they all crowded around the technician, who was cueing up the recording.

"There!" Snyder exclaimed, 'the seniors are entering the pool. There are the boys, the victims, on the pool deck. Follow that boy," Snyder indicated, with his finger on the screen, "he's Case Number One, the one called Wally. And there're numbers Two through Six. All the victims on the bus! Look, Case Number Seven. Please fast forward and keep the focus on the Tiki hut!"

As all of them watched, they could clearly see all the males receiving the oily massages.

"We need to find those two girls and where they came from!" the manager snapped angrily.

"I'm going to call my FBI contact and inform the chairman of the Joint Chiefs of Staff!" Snyder said. "Siribandu, your suspicions might be correct! This is a bioterror attack on our population!'

The young security officer who had arrived while they were fixated on the security footage, looked up at his manager, "I know those girls! They work at the small coffee shop on Jamaican Way and Third Street. I bought a caramel mocha this morning, and they were there!"

Snyder called for the FBI, informing his contact that they had suspects, potentially clues to the current epidemic and biological attack on the country.

In less than thirty minutes, a HAZMAT team, members of the FBI, Florida state police, and local police had surrounded the coffee shop. Twenty guns pointed at the two young girls in custody, no longer in yellow bikinis but clearly terrified. A motorcade was organized and the two girls were separated and loaded into two different FBI vans. Three local motorcycle cops led the block-long line of enforcement vehicles racing toward the interstate and the CDC in Atlanta.

Comment []: I think this needs to be 29. The chapter before, when we are introduced to the girls, is 29

Chapter 26 Interrogation A-Z

April 28, 2018 - 1600 HRS

The motorcycle policemen, lights flashing, stopped all civilian traffic on Clifton Road as the line of vehicles raced through the gates of the CDC. The vans carrying the two girls sped into the parking garage under the facility. The girls, still separated, were escorted to the different interrogation rooms that were dim, windowless, and very cool. The girls sat on metal folding chairs in isolation, each shivering, confused, and scared. One finally screamed out, "Why are you holding us?"

Lee Thomas, lead CIA agent, said, "I believe they're ready to be questioned. Pruden and Soffa, you question the girl in Room Z. Smith and I will conduct the interrogation in the other room. Keep the cameras rolling; the session will be viewed by the Joint Chiefs and the President in the Oval Office. We have got to find who is responsible for making the weaponized lotion!"

Entering Room Z, Pruden offered the girl a coffee and a blanket. "This might make you more comfortable." Taking out a small spiral pad, he sat down behind the plain gray-metal desk next to his partner and asked, "What is your name?"

"Margaret Diaz."

"We're gonna ask you some very important questions that are a matter of national security at the highest level! Your information is vital to the future of our country. Do you understand that you must be cooperative? How is the coffee?"

"Good, I am warming up. Thanks for the blanket," she said, losing the fear in her face as her body relaxed. "Yes, I understand. Although I don't know why you had to bring us all the way here to ask these questions!"

At that moment, Agent Smith pushed open the door hard enough that it slammed against the wall. The lead agent stared with intense eyes that made the young girl's fear return. She continued to shiver.

Smith slammed both fists on the metal table. "Where did you get the lotion?"

Margaret flinched and looked at Agent Thomas. "What is he talking about? I did not do anything bad. Why is he so angry?"

"Answer the man's question," Thomas said softly.

"Look, you little---" Smith hesitated, then continued, "The lotion you used to massage the boys at the pool!"

"Is *that* what this is about? Why didn't you ask us at the Coffee Hut? We could have told you there. A dark-skinned man offered us five hundred dollars to sell the lotion. He said, 'This is a new product and I need it to be promoted.' He emphasized that we should give the free massages to make it sell faster!

"My sister and I don't make five hundred dollars in three days at the coffee shop," Margaret explained, "So we agreed and took the easy money."

"Do you know his name?"

"No! He did not tell us. He said, 'I will meet you back at the Coffee Hut tomorrow at three thirty,' but he never showed. So my sister and I just kept the sales and tips we earned."

"How old was this man?" Smith asked, ignoring the comments about the money.

"Thirty to forty, I think, but it was hard to tell 'cause he had a full beard, sunglasses, and a Tilley hat."

"Did he speak with an accent?" Thomas asked.

"Yeah, like broken English. Kinda seemed Arab-ish, but I'm not sure," the Diaz girl replied.

Meanwhile, in the other room, Catherine Diaz was telling the same story: same amount of money and same description of the salesman.

All agents gathered back in the conference room and compared the new information. Each interrogation team came up with the exact same information. The stories were identical. "We need to find out if the Coffee Hut has security cameras," stated Agent Thomas.

"Is it possible these girls know that they delivered a biological weapon?" wondered Agent Soffa.

"I'm certain they didn't have a clue as to what they were doing," Agent Pruden said with confidence. "They're just two kids trying to get through community college without debt. I used my beauty a few times to pay the electric bill back in college. Surprising how much a sweet innocent smile can get you," Soffa chuckled while Thomas tried to ignore the comment.

"Either way, they must be held in custody. Take them to the upstairs rooms and make sure they are treated like guests. In a short time, we'll know if they're being honest and truly innocent," announced Thomas. "But before they go upstairs, put the two girls together in room Z," he added.

The Diaz sisters, relieved to see each other, sat, pulling the metal chairs closer. "Okay, girls, the lotion you were rubbing on the boys contained a virus that is causing the current epidemic," Soffa revealed. Both girls' eyes widened when they heard the news.

Catherine said, "Oh my God, that horrible disease that is happening to boys?"

"Yes, I'm afraid so," Thomas told them. "You were deceived and it's very possible that you two delivered the first infections of the virus." Both Catherine and Margaret looked at each other and sank into their chairs.

"Sir, we had no idea!" Margaret whined.

"We realize that, but now you can help us. Does the Coffee Hut have a surveillance system?"

"Yes, it does!" Margaret announced. "I'm the one in charge of the system. If you get me back to the Coffee Hut, I can find the footage to help identify the man, ya know, the one that approached Catherine and me about selling the lotion."

"Take these girls to the car, now!" commanded Thomas as he looked at the camera that had been providing images to the President and the other officials. "We've got to identify that bastard!"

Chapter 27   Blake's Blood

April 28, 2018 - 1200 HRS

Leoni pressed the up button on the elevator and turned to Cat. "He is the boldest man I have ever seen. I think Tristan is what Americans call a maverick. You know, real cowboy stuff!"

Smiling and nodding in agreement, Cat replied, "Yeah, true, but when it comes to forensic epidemiology, there's nobody better than Snyder."

"I know, but still… running out of a meeting with the national health secretary?"

"Yeah, only our boss Tristan," Leoni said with a proud smile. "Wonder where he went! Anyway, let's start in the upstairs office."

"Okay."

No sooner did the elevator doors open than they were practically run over by Tristan, rushing out of his office with Blake in his arms. "Guys, help me get Blake to a downstairs quarantine room! I've got to get him into isolation. He has O-type blood. Wes, my brother has B. I'm not sure about Karrie. I still have to find what she has. Until then, Blake must be in total isolation!"

Reaching into his lab coat, Tristan held something out. "Here, put this surgical mask on him and let's take him down the fire escape. Less people steps and we can't take the chance to put Blake in the public elevator!"

> **Comment []:** added this to try to bring the first time we meet Blake use full circle

The boy in his arms stirred and looked up. Since Snyder's brother, Wes, and his wife were celebrating their anniversary, Blake had been with Snyder for the week. They had practiced or watched baseball almost the entire time, including the game cut short by the virus.

"Uncle Tristan, where are you taking me? I want to go home. This place is scary!" Blake whined.

"Blake, you have to trust me. I'll take care of you! I don't want you to get sick."

"Does Mommy know I'm here? She worries too much about me. She doesn't think I'm a big boy who can take care of himself."

As they climbed out the window at the end of the long corridor and stepped out onto the iron fire escape landing, Tristan looked down at his nephew. "Yep, I know you're a big brave dude, but I'm going to call her and make sure she knows you're safe! Do you want to talk to your mom?"

Blake nodded somewhat hesitantly.

Two stories down, Leoni pushed up the window to allow them to exit the fire escape. Still in his arms, Tristan rushed Blake into the quarantine quarters. The air was fresh and the temperature was a cool sixty-six degrees. He placed the small-framed boy onto a stainless steel table; only a sanitary pillow and a thin hospital blanket were there for comfort.

Blake, with a shiver, said, "Uncle Tristan, it's cold in here!"

"I know," his uncle acknowledged as he unfolded another blanket that he took from a clear plastic bag. "Here, put this around you. You'll need to stay in here for a while. I'll turn cartoons on and the Xbox. You'll have your favorite baseball game to play.... all day long, okay?"

"Okay, but don't tell mom," the boy tried to say conspiratorially with a giggle. "Uncle Tristan, you're the coolest!"

"Got you covered, big man! Tristan said with a wink but feeling none of the casualness he was feigning.

Snyder stepped out of the room as air rushed into the decontaminating chamber. Immediately, he pulled his cell out, went to his contacts, and called his brother. "Wes, we have a problem. A very *big* problem!" he said when his brother answered.

"Brother, what did you do this time?" Wes muttered.

Karrie, in the room as well, moved closer to Wes and could hear Tristan. "What happened? Is something wrong with Blake? Oh, my God, please tell me no!"

"Karrie, he's fine right now!" assured Tristan, "But we need to protect him."

"From what?" Wes fired back.

"Haven't you heard about the viral epidemic?!" Snyder asked with deep concern.

Karrie, almost near hysterics, moaned, "*That*?! My God!"

"Relax, will you? I need the two of you to be calm. Blake is okay, but he must be quarantined until I know for sure how to protect him. We need to run some tests; he might be completely immune. It's possible that he's free from getting the contagion. Right now, he's in isolation here at the CDC. He's in the safest place on the planet with the most experienced virologists," Snyder tried to assure them.

"What do you mean – tests?" Wes snapped.

"Wes, Dad was O positive, even though both of us are B type, so Blake might be O as well."

"When will we know?"

"I can test him right here. What is Karrie's blood type?"

Karrie, listening in, spoke into the phone, "I'm A, but what does this all matter?"

Tristan, ignoring her question and scratching his head, asked, "What were your parents?"

"I don't know what Dad was, but Mom got called all the time by the Red Cross. She was what they called a universal donor."

"Then there's a good chance that Blake is O."

Standing there and feeling helpless, Wes insisted, "Why do we need to know?!"

"Wes, the virus is only attacking males with O-type blood! That's why…and I have to go. Please try to stay calm until you hear from me again!"

Tristan hung up the phone, washed and rinsed his hands, and turned to Cat and Leoni. "One of you type Blake's blood…and do it now!"

Chapter 28 Evil Design

April 29, 2018 - 0800 HRS

"The evil bastard has somehow designed an unstoppable biological weapon! The epidemic has been initiated by an intentional release of a highly contagious and weaponized virus. Quibt has created a modern plague, killing more people than the flu epidemic of 1918. The mortality rate is higher than any viral outbreak in history. That fanatical scoundrel has released the biohazard, targeting males, and more specifically, those with O-type blood. He is holding us hostage. The public is now aware of the scheme, and people are protesting on every street corner in every town and city in the country. These radicals are out to destroy the United States, and the attack has escalated to a pandemic, spreading to all continents, even though we know his main target is us. It's obvious that Quibt knows the vulnerability of the global transport infrastructure and is fully aware that we have no way to mitigate this kind of biological threat. What we have feared for years has come to fruition and is now threatening our open society. Transmission is nearly impossible to stop with the current mobile population. The airfare, shipping, and subway systems are defenseless!" General Johnson ended his report to the Joint Chiefs of Staff and the President, standing on the Presidential Great Seal.

"Johnson, what are the options? Do we have any?" asked the President.

"First and foremost, there must be a mandatory quarantine. No one can leave houses, businesses, or schools. Even this will not protect the males since the virus is so small that it penetrates ventilation systems. It is categorized as a Level Four biological threat. As for now, if the individual has O-type blood, he's dead. We have nothing to treat the victims and no vaccine. Our only option is to wait on medical research. That's the only hope."

"Who do we have working on this?" the President asked. "I'm commanding all resources, funds, and medical facilities, or any other needs, to be available to these scientists."

"The best epidemiologists at the CDC, Dr. Snyder and his partners, have found that a tanning oil used in Florida was the primary source of contamination," Johnson added. "Two girls unknowingly spread the virus. They were paid five hundred dollars to rub some kind of tanning oil on a bunch of boys on a class trip to a resort in Florida. From the interrogations, it appears that they were innocent dupes, but they're being held in custody," General Johnson informed the President. "The oil contained the virus! Evidently, this is how the enemy got the biological agent into the country and it was then easily transported by car or truck. Even as we speak, units are investigating, trying to identify the bastard that set up the girls. Hopefully, within the hour, they will be able to review the footage from some coffee shop cameras. The girls confirmed that is where he gave them the tubes of lotion."

The President looked around the room, his face radiating his concern. "Public safety is our number-one priority. We have to find a way to stop the spread. This is a raging forest fire, out of control, and we've got no water to put it out. The sonsabitches have already killed more males than all the losses in the Civil War. All our public health resources must make solving this epidemic the sole focus. Every drug company must make their research resources and staff available. I want the military posted at every biological facility: university labs, hospitals, and every drug company doing research. Is this clear?!"

The group of national leaders simultaneously shouted, "YES, SIR!"

"Where is Dr. Arnold Benedict?! His research at Marshall holds the secret to mRNA manipulation," the National Health Secretary queried the Joint Chiefs.

The President echoed that question: "Where *is* Dr. Benedict? We are wasting time talking. We are losing to Quibt. Our boys are dying in massive numbers. I want this sonofabitch maniac's head on a platter!" the leader of the free world shouted, pounding a fist on the table.

The Secretary of the Navy spoke up for the first time. "Our SEAL team raided Quibt's compound last night in a remote spot in Canada that's since been destroyed. That's where the bastards were holding Benedict hostage for the last three months. We know that Quibt's group tortured Benedict and threatened to kill his daughter to make him give up the genetic technology. They forced him to demonstrate the process for biologically engineering a lethal virus. He suspected, but didn't know for sure, that Quibt's cell was constructing a biological weapon to use against the United States until Benedict overheard a conversation about the current crisis. However, the old professor must still have plenty of fight in him because he told us that he managed to engineer a different virus that wiped out all those with Middle Eastern blood in the compound. He is safe and being debriefed at Fort Detrick."

The President commanded quickly, "Get him now and take him to the CDC to work with Snyder. Maybe these brilliant minds will be able to save us all!" With the President's words still lingering in the air, the entire leadership in the room rose and dashed out through the now-open double doors.

Chapter 29 Breakthrough

April 29, 2018 - 1500 HRS

"It's the Christmas Disease!" Lowenstein shouted as she came running out of her office, nearly knocking Benedict off his feet. Without apology, she turned and made intense eye contact with Snyder. "All symptoms are exactly the same as hemophilia b. When I completed my hematology rotation, I saw several patients with this severe form of hemophilia. It all makes sense!"

"Hey, Cat, take a breath and meet Dr. Arnold Benedict," Snyder said, smiling and shaking his head. "Arnold, meet Dr. Lowenstein."

"Christmas Disease?" asked Benedict, slightly bemused but his frown showing his concern.

"Yes, yes, profuse spontaneous bleeding episodes, factor IX deficiency, nearly diminished in the late stage. Early-onset patients feel pain in the joints and are easily bruised!"

"Dr. Lowenstein, I'm excited to hear your diagnosis. This could signal a huge breakthrough. Do you have it in a report?" Benedict asked.

"No, I just made my diagnosis this morning. I was looking through some old notes from med school, and, unless I'm missing something, all the symptoms add up to the Christmas Disease, known generally as hemophilia b. The Factor IX protein is critically low. The concentrations are less than one percent, which indicates severe hemophilia b. Our gas chromatography readings are indicating the protein initiating the clotting cascade is negligent. We're getting the smallest readings ever recorded for the Factor IX protein. Victims have zero coagulants in their systems."

Snyder added, "Yes, I remember that disorder, it's a mutated F9 gene. It all makes sense. Individuals with this disorder suffer from prolonged bleeding, such as hemarthrosis, bleeding in the joints. All victims align with the diagnosis: spontaneous bleeding episodes into any organ, including the kidneys, stomach, intestines, and brain. Bleeding in the kidneys or stomach and intestines is evidenced by blood in their urine and stool. If I recall correctly, the gene is located on the X chromosome. The disease manifestations are seen most often in males. The males with the smaller paired Y chromosome are virtually defenseless. The F9 gene would be completely exposed to the viral attachment!"

"Yes, all of my records indicate acute hematuria and hematochezia, blood in the stool," Siribandu indicated in support of Lowenstein and Snyder.

"Jesus, Quibt used my knowledge to select males with O-type blood groups in his goal of holding the Western world hostage. He now has the knowledge to threaten with another viral release. He could target any population, race, even gender. It's endless. He has us in a stranglehold, and it doesn't matter about socio-economic status or intellect. Oh, my God, what have I done!?" Benedict moaned, lowering his head and burying his face in his hands.

Snyder, seeing the hopelessness and guilt in Benedict, tried his best to lessen the scientist's burden. "This is a viral chess match. We can beat him with our biological knowledge -- yours, especially! What's been done can be undone by you, with our team's help. That fanatical bastard has nothing on my team!"

"That's right," Siribandu added. "I became a physician to save people, and we are going to save people! Let the military take care of that bastard. By the way, Doctor Benedict, it sounds to me like you have already done your part to stop the attack. You single-handedly took out an entire compound with your knowledge. The good guys need you now, more than ever. Help us stop the epidemic before it becomes a full-blown pandemic."

Dropping his hands and looking back up at the others in the room, Benedict nodded and said, "Enough self-pity. Let's get to your lab!"

In an attempt to ease the tension, Lowenstein said, "Quick, Robin, to the elevator!"

Moments later, as they stepped out of the elevator, Benedict scanned the lab. "Wow, you folks have it all. Must be nice to have an unlimited budget. My state budget would never support a facility this size, let alone the purchase of the equipment to fill it."

Snyder replied, "Yeah, as far as funds are concerned, there have been no limits. The President has provided all resources available for our endeavor. We are the last line of defense. American, and now Canadian, boys are dying by the minute."

Siribandu interrupted. "No time for funding talk. Doctor Benedict, we have lost forty-five thousand males, the majority on the East Coast, but this is changing by the minute. The epidemic began only seven days ago. We are certain that Ground Zero was at that resort and pool in Florida.

"Yes, I was briefed about that on the chopper. Florida, at a resort near that Southern Baptist theme park. If the news was accurate, the first manifestations appeared on the tour bus returning to Virginia, somewhere near the Florida- Georgia line on Interstate 95, correct?"

"Yes, that is true. In addition, an adult male suffered an attack during his stay at the same resort," added Lowenstein. "According to his wife, he also purchased a bottle of the tanning oil. His wife stated that he began bleeding in their room about the same time as the kids at the pool. She could barely complete the interview because her two little boys also had fallen victim to the disease. All three within fifteen minutes."

"That evil bastard! He has crippled America with disease and fear!" Benedict said, shaking his head. "And that poor woman. Her husband and children!"

"Well, she's not the only one in severe bereavement. The entire county is in terror," Siribandu observed, "Science, everyone. We must concentrate. What is the evidence pointing to? Now, with Lowenstein's new evidence, we need a viable hypothesis -- and now!"

Benedict continued to look over his shoulder, still inspecting the lab facility as he walked toward the Level Four quarantine room. On the other side of the large window, Blake took a break from his Mortal Kombat game and peered at his uncle with a smile and a soft wave. Benedict said, "That boy must be the only boy that has survived infection."

"No. He's my nephew, and he's not been exposed," Snyder replied as he waved back at his nephew. He has O-type blood. No one knows that I'm also using the facility to protect him. It is important that you do not tell anyone. You know how the media would love to expose us and make it an us-against-them issue, or start shouting favoritism or abuse of privilege. Heck, if Trump was still around, he'd be screaming that the epidemic was started by the Democrats!"

"Yeah, no doubt any story to increase sales for *The National Enquirer* or improve Fox News' ratings. Sad but true," interjected Lowenstein.

Snyder snapped, "Siribandu, everyone! Doctor Benedict, the young boy who has survived is at Emory University in Atlanta. We did not dare move him to our facility. One reason was the fear of public exposure. The other was, of course, to protect him and secure our facility."

"Yes, yes, of course," Benedict said with an understanding nod. "Emory has one of the best biocontainment hospitals. I would like to visit this young man. In my humble opinion, he definitely is where we need to concentrate our observations and research. If a solution exists, the secret is most likely somewhere in his immune system."

"Okay, then," Snyder announced, "Let's go visit our boy Wally!"

Chapter 30   Wally Blinks

May 4, 2018 - 1100 HRS

Cherie, Ed, Mike, and Dalton stood in the viewing area, looking at Wally connected to tubes and monitor lines. Cherie whispered, "Come on, Wally, you can beat this." Ed and Mike both caressed Cherie's shoulders as they looked down at their friend, who looked like anything but the energetic joker they knew him to be.

Mike said, "Man, does that kid love you. You're all he talks about."

Cherie shook her head sadly. "Some girls told me that, but he never really tried to talk to me. I'd catch him looking at me sometimes, but he'd always turn away."

"He's got a good heart, but he's always been a shy little guy," Dalton said, smiling as Ed stated, "I need to get something to eat. Anyone want to go to the hospital café?"

"Sure, I'll go," Mike replied as he looked at the others. Without further comments, their small group just turned and walked toward the elevators.

Twenty minutes later, Ed stuffed the last French fry into his mouth and announced, "I'm goin' back upstairs." Dalton said, "Well, I'm not. I feel helpless and no good for Wally. I think I'm gonna check out the mall and catch a movie or something."

Mike, making eye contact with Dalton, said, "Yeah, I think I'll go with you. Standin' around is making it worse. I can't just stare at him anymore." Like the others, Cherie looked at Ed, and muttered, "I'm with you, I guess." They all walked towards the elevator. The awkward silence on the ride down seemed to take forever. As they exited the elevator in the lobby, they saw another family that had lost three boys to the disease and were crying and holding onto each other. The fear of death was virtually everywhere. No one, it seemed, could escape the disease. The walls of the elevator had protocol instructions for disease avoidance and precautionary measures. Everywhere they looked, they were reminded of the epidemic.

Returning from more miserable silence in the cafeteria and sweeping the hair out of her face, Cherie stepped out of the elevator and slowly walked toward the viewing area. Peering through the glass, she saw no change in Wally, his skin still bluish with purple spots. The slight up and down movement of his chest gave evidence of his shallow breaths. She pressed her palm against the glass, and her breath began to condense on its cool surface. Still looking into the Level Four containment room, she saw Wally blink. Cherie grabbed Ed's arm and gasped,

"Did you see that?!"

"See what?"

"Wally just blinked! Look, now he's moving his head side to side!" Cherie cried out excitedly.

An attending nurse at the front desk heard the commotion and raced down to the viewing window. "What's going on?"

"Look, see?! Wally's moving his eyes and his head. Is he going to make it?"

"I'll call the response team," the nurse replied with some excitement of her own. Into the hospital phone, the nurse quickly announced, "Patient One is gaining consciousness and making voluntary muscle movements!"

Within a minute, three virology specialists in Level Four suits approached Wally. The one doing the preliminary examination announced, "Involuntary movements are all normal. Steady heartbeat…breathing on his own. Improving voluntary movements. Patient is respondent to periphery reflex test."

Another physician asked, "What is his body temperature?"

"Ninety-nine. That's a four-degree drop in twenty-four hours."

"Wally, can you hear me? How are you feeling?" asked the third physician.

Suddenly opening one eye a crack, Wally shook his head and, lying in the hospital bed, looked up with a brief little smile that belied the agony he was going through. Blinking his eyes rapidly now, he tried to move his hand to his face, but the restricting tubes and line would not allow it.

Another doctor said, "Wally, what is your birthday?"

Opening a very dry mouth, Wally mumbled through equally dry lips, "Uhh…January 26, 2000? Is it my birthday today?"

"Hardly," one doctor replied with a wry smile. "It's the end of April. But you probably will get to celebrate your nineteenth birthday." Turning to a colleague, he instructed, "Contact Snyder! Tell him that Wally is alert and responsive."

"Will do!" the physician said as he rushed to his office to make the call to Snyder's direct line. "Dr. Snyder, this is Dr. David Brown at Emory University. We have good news about Wally. He is fully responsive and all vitals are normal."

"Thank God! Is there any sign of bleeding episodes?" asked Snyder while waving frantically at the other epidemiologists in the white CDC Dodge van.

Brown responded "No! In fact, his Factor IX is reading normal in the thirties."

"What!? How can that be? That means his body has beaten the virus on its own. His cells are winning!" Lowenstein, Siribandu, and Benedict all looked at each other as they sat in the van, listening to Snyder's end of the call. "What could possibly be different about his system? Driver, get us to Emory now!" Snyder ordered with extreme urgency. Minutes later, the white van pulled up in front of the emergency room door. Brown, who was already there to meet them, informed Snyder, "The patient is on the fourth floor. We have all the equipment you need to see Wally."

Nodding briefly, Snyder turned. "Lowenstein, once we're there, pull up Wally's medical history on the quarantine room monitor. Include his past records and, of course, all recordings since the infection of the Christmas Disease."

On the floor above, the vacuum-lock doors closed and the final disinfecting spray misted their bio suits as one by one, they entered the chamber. As they gathered around Wally, Snyder smiled and said, "Doctors, meet Wally, our sole survivor." Siribandu and Lowenstein smiled and looked down.

Benedict nodded his head, and, with a warm greeting, said, "Wally, I think you should pick my lottery ticket numbers! You're the luckiest male with O-type blood on the planet Earth." In little more than a whisper, Wally croaked out, "Okay, if you say so, Dr. Benedict."

Turning to his colleagues, Benedict asked, "What are symptom variances?"

Siribandu reviewed the screen charts and read aloud to the team. "The onset appears to be the same time. On the bus, like the other victims, and the same time as the adult male. Bleeding episode is the same. Initial Factor IX concentrations are same as the others. The difference in his attack is his temperature went to one hundred and six degrees. The others never reached above one hundred and four. In fact, in all other cases, the victims' temperature began to drop after the one hundred and four mark and all were dead at that temperature. Wally's continued to climb for six more hours. Now, within the last twenty-four hours, his temperature has returned to normal. Something in his system is fighting and winning. Metabolic activity is also returning to normal, indicated by the body temperature."

"Very interesting. The human body is a miracle. But there has to be an explanation." Benedict scratched his head and glanced at Siribandu. "Do you have a picture of the virus in this child?"

"No, the images we've been using are from Patients Two, Five and Twelve. I can take one for you, but it will take about an hour. What biome do you want me to use to pull the specimen?" asked Siribandu.

"The bowel region," Benedict said. "I've noticed that Wally had signs of Irritable Bowel Syndrome. He's the only victim that was suffering from an intestinal event during initial infection. Let's start there."

Chapter 31   Why Not Beer?

May 8, 2018

Siribandu and Lowenstein approached the small conference room in the CDC, where Snyder and Benedict were already on a conference call with the President and the other national leaders. Present in the Oval Office were the Secretary of Health, Azar, senior members from the World Health Organization, and General Johnson, all anxious for good news and prepared to implement and enforce any positive protocols to halt the epidemic. Snyder and Benedict looked away briefly from the group of dignitaries on the giant screen and made eye contact with Siribandu, "What're your findings?" asked Snyder. "Do you have a clear image of the virus infecting Wally?" added Benedict.

"Retrovirus?" Snyder asked, overlapping Benedict's question.

"Well, it took a while to find the virus," Siribandu began. "It wasn't floating in the fluids of the bowel region as we first guessed. We had to fractionize a particle in his alimentary canal pathway."

"What do you mean, fractionize?" inquired Benedict with a puzzled look, eyebrows raised high on his wrinkled forehead.

"Because we couldn't find any evidence, we began fractionizing the patient's immune cells and we found not one single virus. We didn't see any evidence of the virus in his platelets, so we began to scan for a cellular anomaly," Lowenstein said. "We prepared and scanned several specimens and then we found something very interesting! Wally has a unique and very large population of *yeast* cells in his large intestine."

Siribandu directed the group's attention to the monitor. "Look, do you see this cell?" she asked, pointing to a round object. "It's not a somatic cell, but it *is* a symbiotic organism in his digestive system. It appears to be a new species of Saccharomycetales."

Snyder interjected, "Yeast?"

"Yes, as I said," Lowenstein replied, supporting her colleague. "I've sequenced the DNA, and it didn't match any recorded yeast species! In fact, the closest related yeast species is only 93% similar to the new yeast's genome."

"It's an entirely new species! The yeast in Wally's system doesn't have a classification," Siribandu announced. "Lowenstein and I fractionized the yeast cells and found the YMe virus in the cells. Somehow, the yeast immobilizes the glycoproteins on the surface of the YMe virus capsid. Interestingly, the glycoproteins embedded in yeast have a greater affinity to the YMe virus. The membranous virus cell structure is less attracted to Wally's platelets' cell membrane than the yeast cell's glycoproteins. In simple terms, Wally's yeast is like a PacMan eating Pac-Dots in the old video game. Because of the greater viral affinity to his yeast, Wally beat the virus! His cells destroy the virus' cells!"

Benedict added, "And his body temperature supports this hypothesis. His immune system was working overtime, and the increased metabolic activity in the yeast production drove his body temperature so high that it killed the virus."

Rubbing his chin, Snyder said, "We might have something here. This is a reasonable explanation for Patient One, but the real question is will it work for all males?" He turned his attention back to the giant monitor. "Mr. President and Mr. Azar, do we have your authorization to immediately try this on humans? Can we inject the new yeast into other infected victims…and can we use it as prophylactic medication for the uninfected, a vaccine?!"

General Johnson exclaimed, "We have to! Men and boys are dying!"

The President nodded.

Snyder jumped from his office chair, running out of the room as the President and other dignitaries watched. Benedict looked at the monitor and then made eye contact with Lowenstein. "Where did he go?" he said in a low voice.

Siribandu just smiled, sighed, and said proudly, "That's my boss!"

Meanwhile, racing out of the elevator to the CDC Level Four biohazard laboratory, Snyder looked frantically for the labeled specimens taken from Wally, thinking, *Where did she put the yeast?"* Looking into the secured biomedical refrigerator, he pulled the sealed test-tube samples labeled *YMe Virus, Patient One*. Quickly, he grabbed an empty sterile flask and made a concentrated solution of glucose. Opening the sample, he poured some of the yeast solution into the glucose and shook the flask vigorously, then, placing the glucose solution in the incubator, set the timer for one hour. After a long impatient wait spent scanning the most recent bits of Lowenstein and Siribandu's notes, Snyder grabbed the potential potion, something that could save his dearly loved nephew. He ran to the quarantine room where Blake was held and instructed his nephew to drink the solution.

Blake took a swallow and then coughed. "Uncle Tristan, this is yucky. It's too sweet! Do I have to drink all of it!?" Blake opened his mouth wide, rolling his tongue from side to side.

"Yes, drink all of it!" Snyder practically shouted, "Please, little man. This can save your life! I need to go back to my office. I'll be back in an hour to take some tests. If all goes as I think it will, I'll be able to call your mom and dad to take you home!"

Racing back downstairs instead of waiting for the elevator, Snyder called his brother on his cell phone, taking the steps two-by-two. "Wes, I think we've found a way to protect Blake from the YMe virus. Time will tell us for sure, but we're almost certain we've got Blake out of harm's way! I'll call you back in an hour. Stay by the phone." Tristan heard Wes yell to Karrie that Blake was going to be okay as he burst back in to rejoin the others.

Meanwhile, back in the conference room, Siribandu, Lowenstein, and Benedict had been discussing the possible distribution problems. "There're millions of doses to be made. No pharmaceutical company can produce the amount needed for the population. There could be riots by those that don't get the vaccine. This could lead our world into total anarchy. What do we do?" the President shouted.

Then Benedict had a Eureka moment: "WHY NOT BEER!?"

All three epidemiologists gasped in unison. Snyder exclaimed, "YES! The yeast vats at the breweries! Every brewery in the country could produce the yeast in infinite numbers once we give them the antiviral yeast. Benedict, the apple just hit you in the head. It's brilliant!"

Lowenstein gasped, "Oh, my gosh! Distribution will be simple with all the beer trucks from here to the West Coast. The logistics are in place already. Every convenience store and liquor store in the Western world can be supplied. Everyone will have access to the yeast because it'll be used to brew the beer. We can have a dose to every American in a week."

Having overheard the entire emotional discussion, the President declared, "Consider it done!"

Chapter 32 The Toast

May 31, 2018 – Memorial Day – 1300 HRS

Back in Virginia, the seniors sat around the pool in Dalton's backyard, basking in the eighty-three-degree day.

"Let's do a toast," Ed suggested as he raised his beer. The rest held their bottles of Why Not Beer high in the air, laughing at each clink as the bottles touched. "To a senior trip to remember and to never forget!" Ed offered as he shook his head from side to side.

"No kiddin', we were the epidemic epicenter!" Mike added from his prone position on the plastic lounge chair. Sitting close to Cherie, Wally smiled from ear to ear, thankful for being alive but even more thankful for being with Cherie, even more than being some kind of national hero.

Dalton slid his *RayBans* down his nose, smirked, and then said, "Wally, who'd have ever believed that your doo doo would someday save the world!?"

The End

Made in the USA
Columbia, SC
22 May 2020